Christopher Marlowe's Edward II: A Retelling

David Bruce

Published by David Bruce, 2022.

Cover Illustration for Christopher Marlowe's *Edward II*: A Retelling

***

A line drawing of King Edward II of England, from *Cassell's History of England*, Century Edition, page 365 — published circa 1902.

***

Educate Yourself
> Read Like A Wolf Eats
> Be Excellent to Each Other
> Books Then, Books Now, Books Forever

***

In this retelling, as in all my retellings, I have tried to make the work of literature accessible to modern readers who may lack some of the knowledge about mythology, religion, and history that the literary work's contemporary audience had.

Do you know a language other than English? If you do, I give you permission to translate this book, copyright your translation, publish or self-publish it, and keep all the royalties for yourself. (Do give me credit, of course, for the original retelling.)

CHRISTOPHER MARLOWE'S EDWARD II: A RETELLING

First edition. July 13, 2022.

Copyright © 2022 David Bruce.

ISBN: 979-8201198817

Written by David Bruce.

Table of Contents

Dedication

Dedicated to Carl Eugene Bruce and Josephine Saturday Bruce

My father, Carl Eugene Bruce, died on 24 October 2013. He used to work for Ohio Power, and at one time, his job was to shut off the electricity of people who had not paid their bills. He sometimes would find a home with an impoverished mother and some children. Instead of shutting off their electricity, he would tell the mother that she needed to pay her bill or soon her electricity would be shut off. He would write on a form that no one was home when he stopped by because if no one was home he did not have to shut off their electricity.

The best good deed that anyone ever did for my father occurred after a storm that knocked down many power lines. He and other linemen worked long hours and got wet and cold. Their feet were freezing because water got into their boots and soaked their socks. Fortunately, a kind woman gave my father and the other linemen dry socks to wear.

My mother, Josephine Saturday Bruce, died on 14 June 2003. She used to work at a store that sold clothing. One day, an impoverished mother with a baby clothed in rags walked into the store and started shoplifting in an interesting way: The mother took the rags off her baby and dressed the infant in new clothing. My mother knew that this mother could not afford to buy the clothing, but she helped the mother dress her baby and then she watched as the mother walked out of the store without paying.

My mother and my father both died at 7:40 p.m.

CAST OF CHARACTERS

Male Characters

King Edward II of England.

Prince Edward: His son. Later, King Edward III.

Edmund, Earl of Kent: King Edward II's half-brother. King Edward II and the Earl of Kent call each other "Brother."

Piers de Gaveston: Later, Earl of Cornwall. Favorite of King Edward II.

Guy, Earl of Warwick.

Thomas, Earl of Lancaster: Queen Isabella's uncle. He greatly dislikes Gaveston because he takes King Edward II's attention away from the Queen.

The Earl of Pembroke.

The Earl of Arundel: King Edward II's ally.

The Earl of Leicester.

The Earl of Berkeley.

Mortimer the elder. In this book he is called Mortimer Senior.

Mortimer the younger: His nephew. In this book he is called Young Mortimer.

Spenser the elder: Later, Earl of Wiltshire and Marquess of Winchester. In this book he is called Spenser Senior.

Spenser the younger: His son. Favorite of King Edward II. Lady Margaret de Clare's attendant. Later, Earl of Gloucester. In this book he is called Young Spenser.

Baldock: a scholar. Tutor to Lady Margaret. Later, King Edward II's Chancellor (Secretary).

The Bishop of Coventry.

The Archbishop of Canterbury.

The Bishop of Winchester.

Lord Beaumont: Supporter of King Edward II.

James: One of Pembroke's men.

Levune: A Frenchman.

Sir John of Hainault: Queen Isabella's ally.

Rice ap Howell: A Welshman. Today, his Welsh first name is more commonly spelled "Rhys."

Mayor of Bristol.

Sir William Trussel: A representative of Parliament.

Sir Thomas Gurney.

Sir John Maltravers.

Lightborn: an assassin.

Three Poor Men.

Herald.

Abbot.

A Mower.

Champion.

Female Characters

Queen Isabella of England: Queen to King Edward II. Sister to King Philip IV of France, aka King Philip the Fair. She is known in history as Isabella of France.

Lady Margaret de Clare: Betrothed to Gaveston. Later, married to him.

Minor Characters

Lords, Ladies, Messengers, Soldiers, Attendants, Monks.

NOTES

King Edward II's life dates are 25 April 1284 – 21 September 1327.

King Edward II reigned 8 July 1307 – 20 January 1327. He was deposed 20 January 1327.

King Edward III's life dates are 13 November 1312 – 21 June 1377.

King Edward III reigned 25 January 1327 – 21 June 1377.

One of King Edward III's sons was Edward the Black Prince.

Lightborn: The name is a translation of Lucifer.

Queen Isabella was French. She was King Philip IV of France's sole daughter, and she had three brothers who became Kings of France: Charles IV, Philip V, and Louis X. They were of the House of Capet; the House of Valois was a related house. Queen Isabella's cousin, Philip of Valois, became King Philip VI of France, succeeding Charles IV. Marlowe made a mistake in this play when he identified King Charles IV of France as being of the House of Valois. The word "House" means "Family."

King Philip IV of France is also known as Philip the Fair.

Killingworth Castle is known today as Kenilworth Castle.

In this culture, a man of higher rank would use words such as "thee" and "thy" to refer to a servant. However, two close friends or a husband and wife could properly use "thee," "thy," "thine," and "thou" to refer to each other.

Words such as "you" and "your" were more formal and respectful.

"Sirrah" was used to refer to a male of lower status, such as a servant, than the speaker. However, a father could properly call a son "Sirrah."

PREFACE

Since boyhood, King Edward II and Gaveston had been friends. When Edward II was just a Prince, he asked his father, King Edward I of England, to give the Frenchman Gaveston valuable land in France as a gift. This enraged King Edward I, and he banished Gaveston to Gaveston's home in Gascony on 26 February 1307.

On 7 July 1307, King Edward I died, and on 25 February 1308, King Edward II had his coronation. Even before that, in August 1307, Edward II recalled his friend Gaveston from exile.

As the play opens, Gaveston is re-reading a letter from Edward II that recalls him from exile.

Quickly, we learn that the relationship between King Edward II and Gaveston is more than platonic.

CHAPTER 1

— 1.1 —

[Scene 1]

Gaveston stood on a street in London as he re-read a letter from King Edward II.

He read out loud: "*My father is deceased. Come, Gaveston, and share the kingdom with thy dearest friend.*"

Gaveston then said, "Ah, words that fill me completely with delight! What greater bliss can happen to Gaveston than to live and be the favorite of a King!

"Sweet Prince, I come! These, these amorous lines of thine might have forced me to have swum from France, and, like Leander, gasped upon the sand, as long as thou would smile, and take me in thine arms."

Gaveston was using words such as "thou," "thy," and "thine" to refer to King Edward II. These pronouns were the kind that intimate friends or married couples would use to refer to each other.

In Greek mythology, Leander was a man who loved the woman Hero. Leander swam across the Hellespont each night to visit her. She lit a lamp each night to guide his way across the narrow sea. One night, the winds blew out Hero's light, and Leander drowned. When Hero saw her lover's dead body, she committed suicide.

The modern name for the Hellespont is the Dardanelles.

Gaveston continued, "The sight of London to my exiled eyes is as Elysium to a newly come soul."

Elysium is the part of the Land of the Dead that is reserved for people who have led good lives. It is a pleasant place to be.

He continued, "It is like Elysium not because I love the city of London or the men, but because it harbors him I hold so dear — the King, upon whose bosom let me die, and with the world be still at enmity."

In this culture, "to die" means "to orgasm" as well as "to faint," in addition to its most common meaning.

Gaveston continued, "What need do the Arctic people have to love starlight, when to them the Sun shines both by day and by night?"

During the summer in the Arctic, the Sun never sets and so the people of the Arctic need no starlight.

Metaphorically, the Sun is King Edward II, who shines on Gaveston. The stars that give starlight are the lordly peers, aka nobles. Because the Sun always shines on Gaveston, he has no need for the stars.

Gaveston continued:

"Farewell, base stooping to the lordly peers — I have no need to bow to them. My knee shall bow to none but to the King.

"As for the multitude of people, who are but sparks, raked up in embers of their poverty, *tanti!*"

As he said "*tanti!*," which means "So much for you!" he made a rude gesture. He had little or no respect for the common people — for them to show even a spark of life, they had to be metaphorically raked like embers that had been covered with ashes in order not to go out at night.

He continued, "I'll first fan and fawn on the wind, which glances at and glides off my lips, and flies away, before I'll flatter the nobles."

Gaveston believed that he could control and manipulate the common people. By fawning on — that is, flattering — them, he could fan their embers into a fire.

He then asked himself, "But what is this now? Who are these men coming toward me?"

Three poor men walked over to Gaveston.

The poor men answered the question: "We are such men as desire your worship's service. We want to work for you."

"What can thou do?" Gaveston asked the first poor man.

"I can ride," the first poor man answered.

"But I have no horses," Gaveston said, and then he asked the second poor man, "Who are thou?"

"A traveller," the second poor man answered.

"Let me see," Gaveston said. "Thou would do well to wait on me as I eat, and entertain me by telling me lies of the kind travelers tell, and if I like your stories, I'll hire you."

He then asked the third poor man, "And who are thou?"

"A soldier who has served in the campaigns against the Scot — Robert Bruce," the third poor man said.

King Edward I fought many campaigns against the Scots, including Robert Bruce and William Wallace. He was known as the Hammer of the Scots. Many disabled soldiers became beggars after the wars ceased.

Gaveston said, "Why, there are hospitals for such as you. I have no war, and therefore, sir, be gone."

The kind of "hospital" he meant was a charitable institution for poor and disabled soldiers as well as other poor and ill people.

"Farewell, and perish by a soldier's hand, you who would reward them with a hospital!" the third poor man said.

Gaveston said quietly to himself, "Yes, yes, these words of his move me as much as if a goose should play the porcupine and shoot her plumes at me, thinking to pierce my breast."

In this culture, people believed that porcupines could shoot their quills as if they were darts. If a goose were to shoot its feathers at Gaveston, the feathers were unlikely to cause much damage.

Gaveston added quietly to himself, "But yet it is no difficulty to speak fair words to men. I'll flatter these men, and make them live in hope."

He then said out loud to the three poor men, "You know that I recently came out of France, and I have not yet seen my lord the King. If all goes well, I'll give all of you a job."

"We thank your worship," the three poor men said.

"I have some business," Gaveston said. "Leave me to myself."

"We will wait here about the court," the three poor men replied.

Everyone except Gaveston exited.

"Do wait here about the court," Gaveston said. "These are not men for me. I must have wanton poets who write about lascivious love, pleasant wits, musicians who with the touching of a string may draw the pliable King whichever way I please. Music and poetry are his delight. Therefore, for the King I'll arrange Italian masques to be performed at night."

Masques are short entertainments, usually with music and dancing.

He continued, "I'll also have sweet speeches, comedies, and pleasing shows; and during the day, when he shall walk outside, my pages shall be clad like forest nymphs."

Pages are young male servants.

Gaveston continued, "My men, like half-man, half-goat, and all-horny satyrs grazing on the lawns, shall with their goat feet dance old-fashioned country dances. Sometimes a lovely boy in the shape of Diana, goddess of virginity and the hunt, with hair that gilds — covers in gold — the water as it glides, bracelets of pearl about his naked arms, and in his playful hands an olive branch, to hide those parts that men delight to see, shall bathe himself in a spring; and there, hard by" — besides the risqué meaning, 'hard' means 'close' — "another boy costumed like Actaeon, peeping through the grove, shall by the angry goddess be transformed, and running in the likeness of a stag and pulled down by yelping hounds, he shall seem to die."

While hunting with his hounds, the Theban Actaeon unintentionally saw Diana bathing naked in a pool of water. Diana, a goddess who was fiercely protective of her virginity, turned him into a stag with a human mind, and then his hunting hounds picked up his scent, chased and caught him, and ripped him to pieces.

The goddess Diana's Greek name is Artemis.

Gaveston continued, "Such things as these best please his majesty."

He heard a sound, looked in that direction, and said, "My lord! Here comes the King and the nobles from the Parliament. I'll stand to the side without being seen and listen to what they say."

King Edward II, the Earl of Lancaster, Mortimer Senior, Young Mortimer; Edmund, Earl of Kent (Edward II's half-brother); Guy, the Earl of Warwick; the Earl of Pembroke, other lords, and many attendants entered.

The Earl of Lancaster, Mortimer Senior, Young Mortimer, and the Earl of Warwick were all opposed to Gaveston returning to England. They had been discussing this with King Edward II.

"Lancaster!" King Edward II said.

"My lord," the Earl of Lancaster answered.

Unseen and unheard, Gaveston said quietly to himself, "I abhor that Earl of Lancaster."

The Earl of Lancaster also abhorred Gaveston.

"Will you not grant me this?" King Edward II asked.

He said quietly to himself, "In spite of them, I'll have what I want, and these two Mortimers, who cross and obstruct me thus, shall know I am displeased."

"If you love us, my lord, hate Gaveston," Mortimer Senior said.

Gaveston said quietly to himself, "That villain Mortimer! I'll be his death."

Young Mortimer, whose uncle was Mortimer Senior, said, "My uncle here, and this Earl of Lancaster, and I myself swore to your father, King Edward I, at his death, that Gaveston should never return into the realm.

"And know, my lord, that before I will break my oath this sword of mine, which should fight off your foes, shall sleep within the scabbard at thy need, and underneath thy banners let march who will, for Young Mortimer will hang up his armor."

Young Mortimer was saying that he would refuse to fight for King Edward II if England were invaded — unless Gaveston remained banished from England. In saying that, he switched from the respectful word "your" to the less respectful word "thy."

Gaveston said quietly to himself, "*Mort dieu!*"

"*Mort dieu!*" means "By God's death!"

"Well, Young Mortimer, I'll make thee regret these words," King Edward II said. "Is it fitting for thee to contradict thy King?

"Do thou frown at your King, aspiring, ambitious Lancaster? The sword shall plane the furrows of thy brows and make them completely flat, and hew these knees of yours that now are grown so stiff and make them bend so that you can kneel before me.

"I will have Gaveston, and you shall know what danger it is to stand against your King."

"Well done, Ned!" Gaveston said quietly to himself.

"Ned" is a nickname for "Edward." Gaveston was close enough to Edward II to refer to him by a nickname.

"My lord, why do you thus incense your peers, who by their nature and their high birth and social status would love and honor you, except for that base and obscure lowly born Gaveston?" the Earl of Lancaster said. "I have four Earldoms besides the Earldom of Lancaster: I have the Earldoms of Derby, Salisbury, Lincoln, and Leicester.

"These four Earldoms I will sell to give my soldiers pay, before Gaveston shall stay within the realm. Therefore, if he has returned to England, expel him immediately."

The Earl of Lancaster was threatening to rebel ("give my soldiers pay") if Gaveston were not exiled again.

The Earl of Kent, who was King Edward II's half-brother, said, "Barons and Earls, your pride has made me mute and speechless. But now I'll speak, and to the irrefutable point, I hope. I remember, in the days of my father, Lord Percy of the North, being highly angry, insulted and challenged Mowbray in the presence of the King. For this act, had not his highness loved him well, he should have lost his head; but with a single look from his King the undaunted spirit of Percy was pacified, and Mowbray and he were reconciled. Yet you dare oppose the King to his face."

He then said to King Edward II, "Brother, revenge it, and let the heads of these men preach upon poles for the trespass of their tongues."

Traitors to the King were often drawn, hanged, and quartered. They were drawn on a wagon to the place of execution, hanged, and then cut into four quarters. After all this, their heads were cut off and placed on the tops of poles to be displayed in public as a warning to others who might think about becoming a traitor.

"Oh, our heads!" the Earl of Warwick exclaimed.

"Yes, yours," King Edward II said, "and therefore I would wish you to consent to Gaveston's returning to England."

The Earl of Warwick said quietly to Young Mortimer, "Bridle your anger, gentle Mortimer."

Young Mortimer replied, "I cannot, and I will not. I must speak."

He said to King Edward II, to whom he was distantly related, "Cousin, our hands I hope shall defend our heads, and strike off the head of that man — Gaveston — who makes you threaten us."

In this society, the word "cousin" was used with a wider meaning than it has now. It was used to refer to many kinds of familial relationships.

Young Mortimer then said to Mortimer Senior, "Come, uncle, let us leave the brainsick King, and henceforth parley with our naked swords. Our swords will do the talking."

"The Welch populace has men enough to save our heads," Mortimer Senior said.

"All Warwickshire will love Gaveston for my sake," the Earl of Warwick said sarcastically.

"And in the north of England, Gaveston has many friends," the Earl of Lancaster said sarcastically.

He added, "Adieu, my lord, and either change your mind, or look to see the throne, where you should sit, float in blood, and see the fawning, flattering head of thy base minion — Gaveston — thrown at thy lovesick head."

"Minion" has these meanings: 1) a favorite, and 2) a homosexual lover.

Everyone exited except King Edward II, the Earl of Kent, the still-unseen Gaveston, and the King's guards.

"I cannot endure these haughty threats," Edward II said. "Am I a King, and must be overruled?"

He added, "Brother, display my battle ensigns in the field of battle. I'll bandy — exchange blows — with the Barons and the Earls, and either die or live with Gaveston."

"I can no longer keep myself from my lord," Gaveston said, coming out of hiding.

Seeing him, King Edward II said, "What! Gaveston, welcome."

Gaveston knelt and kissed the King's hand: This was a formal greeting to a King.

"Don't kiss my hand," King Edward II said as he hugged Gaveston. "Embrace me, Gaveston, as I do thee. Why should thou kneel before me? Don't thou know who I am?

"I am thy friend, thy other self, another Gaveston.

"Hylas was not more mourned by Hercules than thou has been mourned by me since thy exile."

Hercules and Hylas, a youth who served as Hercules' armor-bearer and page, sailed on the *Argo* with Jason in search of the Golden Fleece. Some water nymphs abducted Hylas, and he was never seen again. Distraught, Hercules searched a long time for Hylas, and the *Argo* sailed on without them.

Gaveston said, "And, since I was exiled from here, no soul in Hell has felt more torment than poor Gaveston."

"I know it," King Edward II said.

He said to the Earl of Kent, his half-brother, "Brother, welcome my friend home."

He then said to Gaveston, "Now let the treacherous Mortimers conspire, as well as that arrogant and proud-minded Earl of Lancaster. I have my wish in that I enjoy thy sight, and sooner shall the sea overwhelm my land than bear the ship that shall transport thee hence.

"I here create thee Lord High Chamberlain, Chief Secretary to the state and me, Earl of Cornwall, and King and Lord of Man."

King and Lord of Man referred to the Isle of Man, whose ruler had some authority like that of the King of England. "Lord of Man" may also include a reference to homosexuality since wives in this culture called their husbands "lord."

"My lord, these titles far exceed my worth," Gaveston said.

The Earl of Kent agreed with Gaveston. He said to King Edward II, "Brother, the least of these titles may well suffice for one of greater birth than Gaveston."

He meant that just one of these titles, and that one the least valuable title, would be more than enough to satisfy a person with a better birth and higher social status than Gaveston.

"Cease, brother, for I cannot bear these words," King Edward II said to the Earl of Kent.

He then said to Gaveston, "Thy worth, sweet friend, is far above my gifts to you. Therefore, to equal your worth, receive my heart. If for these high titles thou should be hated, I'll give thee more, for only to honor thee is Edward pleased with kingly authority.

"Do thou fear that thou are not safe? Thou shall have a guard.

"Do thou lack gold? Go to my treasury.

"Would thou be loved and feared? Receive my seal, save or condemn and in our name command whatsoever thy mind desires or fancy likes."

King Edward II was giving Gaveston immense authority: He could pardon or punish people as he wished, and he could make any orders he wanted to in the King's name!

"It shall be enough for me to enjoy your love," Gaveston said. "As long I have it, I think myself as great as Caesar riding in the Roman street with captive Kings walking behind his triumphant chariot."

The Bishop of Coventry entered the room.

King Edward II and the Bishop of Coventry had a history. In June 1305, the Bishop of Coventry had criticized Edward — then a Prince because his father the King was still living — for invading his woods. King Edward I sided with the Bishop of Coventry, who was his Treasurer, and he banished his son the Prince from the royal court for six months.

"Where goes my lord of Coventry so fast?" King Edward II asked.

"To celebrate your father's funeral rites," the Bishop of Coventry answered.

King Edward I died on 7 July 1307. His body was taken to Waltham Abbey, and he was not buried at Westminster Abbey until 27 October 1307.

"But has that wicked Gaveston returned?" the Bishop of Coventry asked, seeing Gaveston.

"Yes, priest, and he lives to be revenged on thee, who was the only cause of his exile," King Edward II said.

King Edward I had exiled Gaveston on 26 February 1307; the Bishop of Coventry had been then and for some time the King's most trusted advisor.

"That is true," Gaveston said, "and, but for reverence of these robes — these vestments — of thine, thou should not step one foot beyond this place. In other words, if you weren't a Bishop, you would suffer my revenge."

"I did no more than I was bound to do," the Bishop of Coventry said. "And, Gaveston, unless thou be morally reformed, then, just as I did previously incite the Parliament, so will I now, and thou shall go back to France."

Gaveston said sarcastically, "Saving your reverence, you must pardon me."

In this society, people said "saving your reverence" to a superior when they were about to say something that might cause offence. Often, people used "sir-reverence" for "saving your reverence." Another meaning of "sir-reverence" is "human excrement," which is something that could be found in some channels.

"Throw off his golden miter, tear his stole, and in the channel christen him anew," King Edward II said as Gaveston grabbed the Bishop of Coventry.

A miter is the tall headdress that a Bishop wears. A stole is a vestment that a Bishop wears over the shoulders. A channel could be a street-gutter or an open sewer, or both combined.

"Ah, brother, lay not violent hands on him," the Earl of Kent said. "For he'll complain to the Holy See."

He meant that the Bishop of Coventry would complain to the Pope.

"Let him complain to the See of Hell!" Gaveston said. "I'll be revenged on him for my exile."

"No, spare his life, but seize upon his goods — his property and possessions," King Edward II advised. "Be thou Lord Bishop, and receive his rents — his income — and make him serve thee as thy chaplain. I give him to thee; here, treat him as thou will."

"He shall go to prison, and there die in shackles," Gaveston said.

"Yes, to the Tower of London, the Fleet Prison, or wherever thou wish," King Edward II said.

"For this offense be thou accursed and excommunicated by God!" the Bishop of Coventry said.

King Edward II asked loudly, "Who's there?"

This was a way to summon attendants and guards. Some guards came over to the King.

He then ordered, "Convey this priest to the Tower of London."

"True, true!" the Bishop of Coventry said.

One meaning of the word "convey" was "steal." The King was basically kidnapping the Bishop of Coventry and putting him in the Tower of London. In addition, the King was stealing the Bishop of Coventry's wealth. "Conveyance" means "transfer of property."

The Bishop of Coventry exited under guard.

"But in the meantime, Gaveston, leave, and take possession of his house and goods," King Edward II said. "Come, follow me, and thou shall have my body of guards to see it done, and bring thee safely back again."

"What should a priest do with so beautiful a house?" Gaveston said. "A prison may be more fitting and appropriate for his holiness."

The Bishop of Coventry was a very wealthy man, although saints such as Francis courted Lady Poverty by taking a vow of poverty. Religious people have often spent time in prison or have lived in small cells.

— 1.2 —

[Scene 2]

Mortimer Senior and Young Mortimer met the Earl of Warwick and the Earl of Lancaster. They talked together.

"It is true," the Earl of Warwick said. "The Bishop of Coventry is in the Tower, and his goods and body have been given to Gaveston."

"What!" the Earl of Lancaster said. "Will they tyrannize upon the Church?"

King Edward II was acting like a tyrant over the Church because he had imprisoned the Bishop of Coventry.

The Earl of Lancaster continued, "Ah, wicked King! Accursed Gaveston! This ground, which is corrupted with their steps, shall be their untimely sepulcher or mine. Someone will die for this!"

"Well, let that spiteful, troublesome, foolish Frenchman Gaveston securely guard himself," Young Mortimer said. "Unless his breast is sword proof, he shall die."

"What is this?" Mortimer Senior said, looking at the Earl of Lancaster. "Why is the Earl of Lancaster drooping?"

The Earl of Lancaster was unhappy and depressed. So was the Earl of Warwick.

"Why is Guy of Warwick discontent?" Young Mortimer asked.

The Earl of Warwick's given name was Guy.

"That villain Gaveston has been made an Earl," the Earl of Lancaster answered.

Gaveston was a gentleman, but an Earl ranks much higher than a gentleman. Becoming the Earl of Cornwall was a major rise in social status for Gaveston.

"An Earl!" Mortimer Senior said.

"Yes," the Earl of Warwick said, "and in addition he has been made Lord Chamberlain of the Realm, and Secretary, too, and Lord of Man."

"We may not nor will we tolerate this," Mortimer Senior said.

"Why don't we ride posthaste from here to levy men and raise an army?"
Young Mortimer asked.

The Earl of Lancaster said, "He must be called 'My Lord of Cornwall' now
every time he is addressed."

After making Gaveston the Earl of Cornwall, King Edward II had decreed
that Gaveston must be addressed by the title "Lord of Cornwall."

The Earl of Lancaster added, "And happy is the man whom Gaveston
grants, in return for removing his hat to show him respect, one good look. Thus,
arm in arm, the King and Gaveston do march. Nay, more, the guard waits upon
his lordship — Gaveston — and all the court begins to flatter him."

"Thus leaning on the shoulder of the King," the Earl of Warwick said, "he
nods and scorns and smiles at those who pass."

"Does no man object to the slave?" Mortimer Senior asked.

"All resent him, but none dares speak a word," the Earl of Lancaster
answered.

"Ah, that reveals their baseness, Earl of Lancaster!" Young Mortimer said.
"If all the Earls and Barons thought as I do, we'd drag Gaveston from the bosom
of the King, and at the court gate we'd hang up the peasant, who, swollen with
the venom of ambitious pride, will be the ruin of the realm and us."

The Archbishop of Canterbury and one of his attendants entered the scene.

"Here comes his grace my Lord of Canterbury," the Earl of Warwick said.

"His countenance reveals that he is displeased," the Earl of Lancaster said.

The Archbishop of Canterbury talked to his attendant about what had
happened to the Bishop of Coventry: "First, his sacred garments were torn, and
then they laid violent hands upon him. Next, he was imprisoned, and his goods
seized. This certify the Pope. Leave, take a horse."

To "certify" the Pope meant to give the Pope certain — known to be true
— information.

The attendant exited.

"My lord, will you take arms against the King?" the Earl of Lancaster asked.

"Why need I do that?" the Archbishop of Canterbury said. "God himself
is up in arms when violence is offered to the Church."

"Then will you join with us, who are the King's peers, to banish or behead
that Gaveston?" Young Mortimer asked.

The peers were nobles.

"What else, my lords?" the Archbishop of Canterbury said. "Of course I will. For it closely concerns me: The diocese of Coventry is his — Gaveston is now the Bishop of Coventry."

Queen Isabella entered the scene.

"Madam, to where is your majesty walking so fast?" Young Mortimer asked.

Her husband, King Edward II, who preferred to spend time with Gaveston, cruelly neglected Queen Isabella.

Queen Isabella answered, "To the forest, gentle Mortimer, to live in grief and wretched discontent; for now my lord the King regards me not, but dotes upon the love of Gaveston."

"To the forest" means "to the wilderness." She was using the phrase metaphorically to mean that she would seclude herself.

Queen Isabella continued, "The King pats Gaveston's cheeks and hangs about his neck, smiles in his face, and whispers in his ears, and when I come, he frowns, as if to say to me, 'Go wherever thou will, seeing I have Gaveston.'"

"Isn't it strange that he is thus bewitched?" Mortimer Senior asked.

"Madam, return to the court again," Young Mortimer said. "That sly, deceiving, inveigling Frenchman we'll exile, or lose our lives, and yet, before that day shall come, the King shall lose his crown; for we have power, and courage, too, to be revenged at full."

"But yet do not lift your swords against the King," the Archbishop of Canterbury said.

"No, but we'll lift Gaveston away from here," the Earl of Lancaster said.

"To lift" means "to steal," but there was an implied threat of lifting Gaveston after placing a rope around his neck.

"And war must be the means of removing Gaveston, or he'll stay in England always," the Earl of Warwick said.

"Then let him stay; for, rather than that my lord and husband shall be oppressed by civil mutinies, I will endure a melancholy life," Queen Isabella said, "and let the King frolic with his minion."

"My lords, to ease all this, only hear me speak," the Archbishop of Canterbury said. "We and the rest, who are the King's counselors, will meet, and with a general consent confirm Gaveston's banishment with our hands and seals.

"What we confirm, the King will frustrate by annulling it," the Earl of Lancaster predicted.

"Then we may lawfully revolt from him," Young Mortimer said.

"But say, my lord, where shall this meeting be?" the Earl of Warwick asked.

"At the New Temple, home of the military order the Templars," the Archbishop of Canterbury answered.

"I am happy with that," Young Mortimer said.

"And in the meantime," the Archbishop of Canterbury said, "I'll entreat you all to cross the Thames River and go to the Palace of Lambeth, and stay there with me."

The Palace of Lambeth was the London residence of the Archbishop of Canterbury.

"Come, then, let's go," the Earl of Lancaster said.

"Madam, farewell," Young Mortimer said to the Queen.

"Farewell, sweet Mortimer," Queen Isabella said, "and, for my sake, don't recruit soldiers to fight against the King."

"Yes, if words will serve," Young Mortimer said. "If words will not serve, then I must recruit soldiers."

— 1.3 —
[Scene 3]

Gaveston and the Earl of Kent talked together. Gaveston was on close enough terms with the Earl of Kent that he could call him by his given name: Edmund.

"Edmund, know that the mighty Prince of Lancaster, who has more Earldoms than an ass can bear, and both the Mortimers, two goodly men" — he was being sarcastic — "along with Guy of Warwick, that fearsome knight, have gone towards Lambeth. There let them remain."

— 1.4 —
[Scene 4]

The Earl of Lancaster, the Earl of Warwick, the Earl of Pembroke, Mortimer Senior, Young Mortimer, and the Archbishop of Canterbury talked together.

"Here is the formal document for Gaveston's exile," the Earl of Lancaster said to the Archbishop. "May it please your lordship to sign your name?"

"Give me the paper," the Archbishop of Canterbury said.

"Quick, quick, my lord," the Earl of Lancaster said. "I long to write my name."

The Archbishop of Canterbury signed his name, and the others signed their names after him.

"But I long more to see him banished from here," the Earl of Warwick said.

"The name of Mortimer shall frighten the King, unless he be turned away from that base peasant," Young Mortimer said.

King Edward II, Gaveston, and the Earl of Kent arrived upon the scene.

"What! Are you angered that Gaveston sits next to me?" King Edward II said. "It is our will and pleasure; we will have it so."

Normally, the Queen would sit by the King.

"Your grace does well to place him by your side, for nowhere else is the new Earl — Gaveston — so safe," the Earl of Lancaster said.

"What man of noble birth can endure this sight?" Mortimer Senior said. "*Quam male conveniunt!*"

This is Latin for "How badly they go together!" One reason he meant for this was that Edward II was the son of a King, while Gaveston was merely the son of a French knight. Another reason was that they were a homosexual couple.

He added, "See what a scornful, contemptuous look the peasant casts."

"Can kingly lions fawn on creeping ants?" the Earl of Pembroke asked.

"Ignoble vassal, who, like Phaëthon, aspires to the guidance of the Sun!" the Earl of Warwick said.

Phaëthon went to his father, the god Apollo, and asked to be allowed to drive the Sun-chariot across the sky and bring light to the world. But Phaëthon was unable to control the stallions, and they ran wildly away with the Sun-chariot, wreaking havoc and destruction upon Humankind and the world by making the chariot come so close to the Earth that it scorched the Earth. The King of the gods, Jupiter, saved Humankind and the world by throwing a thunderbolt at Phaëthon and killing him.

Phaëthon overreached himself, and the Earl of Warwick was saying that Gaveston was overreaching himself. Just as Phaëthon fell, so would Gaveston fall.

"Their downfall is at hand, their forces down," Young Mortimer said. "We will not thus be bullied and overpeered and scorned."

"Overpeered" means "looked down on" and "condescended to."

"Lay hands upon that traitor Young Mortimer!" King Edward II ordered.

"Lay hands upon that traitor Gaveston!" Mortimer Senior ordered.

King Edward II's order was ignored, but several followers of Mortimer Senior obeyed his order. Many swords were drawn in the process.

"Is this the duty that you owe your King?" the Earl of Kent asked.

"We know our duties," the Earl of Warwick said about the King. "Let him know his peers."

"Where will you take him?" King Edward II demanded. "Stay, or you shall die."

"We are no traitors; therefore, don't threaten us," Mortimer Senior said.

"No, don't threaten them, my lord, but pay them back and punish them as they deserve," Gaveston said. "If I were a King —"

"Thou, peasant!" Young Mortimer interrupted. "Why do you talk about being a King, you who are barely a gentleman by birth?"

Gaveston was the son of a French knight and therefore a gentleman, but Earls much outranked knights.

"Even if he were a peasant, I'll make the proudest of you stoop and bow down to him because he is my minion," King Edward II said.

"My lord, you may not thus disparage and dishonor us," the Earl of Lancaster said.

He ordered, "Away, I say, with hateful Gaveston! Take him away!"

"And away with the Earl of Kent, who favors him," Mortimer Senior said.

Guards took Gaveston and the Earl of Kent away.

King Edward II said, "Nay, then, lay violent hands upon your King!

"Here, Young Mortimer, sit thou in Edward's throne.

"Warwick and Lancaster, you wear my crown.

"Was ever any King thus overruled as I am?"

"Learn, then, to rule us and the realm better," the Earl of Lancaster said.

"What we have done, our heart blood shall maintain," Young Mortimer said. "We will defend with our blood what we have done."

"Do you think that we can endure this upstart pride?" the Earl of Warwick asked the King.

"Anger and wrathful fury stops my speech," King Edward II replied. "I am speechless."

"Why are you angry?" the Archbishop of Canterbury asked the King. "Be patient, my lord, and see what we your counselors have done."

"My lords, now let us all be resolute, and either have our wills, or lose our lives," Young Mortimer said.

This was an important moment. If the lords don't get what they want now, they may be judged traitors and lose their lives.

"Did you meet for this, you proud foolhardy peers?" King Edward II asked. "Before my sweet Gaveston shall part from me, this isle shall float upon the ocean, and wander to the unfrequented India."

"You know that I am the representative of the Pope," the Archbishop of Canterbury said. "On your allegiance to the See of Rome, subscribe, as we have done, to his exile. Sign this formal document of exile."

"Excommunicate the King, if he refuses to sign," Young Mortimer said, "and then we can depose him, and elect another King."

To excommunicate someone means to cut them off from the sacraments, such as communion, of the Church, and to cut them off from church services and religious rites. In the case of the King, it also means to release the King's subjects from any duty and loyalty to him.

"Aye, there it goes!" King Edward II said. "But yet I will not yield. Curse me, depose me, do the worst you can."

"Then do not delay, my lord," the Earl of Lancaster said to the Archbishop of Canterbury, "but do it immediately."

The Archbishop of Canterbury said to King Edward II, "Remember how the Bishop of Coventry was abused. Either banish the man — Gaveston — who was the cause of the abuse, or I will immediately discharge these lords of all duty and allegiance due to thee."

The Catholic Church claimed the authority to release a King's subjects from their duty and allegiance to their King. Such subjects need no longer be loyal to the King.

King Edward II said quietly to himself, "It is useless for me to threaten them; I must speak fair words to them."

He said out loud, "The representative of the Pope will be obeyed."

He then attempted to bribe his nobles with high offices:

"My lord Archbishop of Canterbury, you shall be Chancellor of the Realm.

"Thou, Lancaster, shall be High Admiral of our fleet.

"Young Mortimer and his uncle shall be Earls.

"And you, lord Warwick, shall be President of the North.

"And thou, Earl of Pembroke, shall be President of Wales.

"If this does not make you content, make separate kingdoms of this monarchy, and share it equally among you all, so I may have some nook or corner left to frolic with my dearest Gaveston."

The President of the North is the King's Deputy in the North. The President of Wales is the King's Deputy in Wales.

"Nothing shall alter us," the Archbishop of Canterbury said. "We are resolved."

"Come, come, sign the formal document of exile," the Earl of Lancaster said.

"Why should you love him whom the world hates so?" Young Mortimer asked.

"Because he loves me more than all the world," King Edward II said. "Ah, none but uncivilized and savage-minded men would seek the ruin of my Gaveston. You who are nobly born should pity him."

"You who are princely born should shake him off," the Earl of Warwick said. "For shame, sign the document of exile, and let the scoundrel depart."

"Urge him, my lord," Mortimer Senior said to the Archbishop of Canterbury.

"Do you agree to banish Gaveston from the realm?" the Archbishop of Canterbury asked the King.

"I see that I must, and therefore I agree," King Edward II said. "Instead of ink, I'll write my signature with my tears."

"The King is lovesick for his minion," Young Mortimer said.

King Edward II signed the formal document of exile.

"It is signed," King Edward II said, "and now, accursed hand, fall off!"

"Give the document to me," the Earl of Lancaster said. "I'll have it proclaimed in the streets."

"I'll see Gaveston immediately dispatched away," Young Mortimer said.

"Now is my heart at ease," the Archbishop of Canterbury said.

"And so is mine," the Earl of Warwick said.

"This will be good news to the common people," the Earl of Pembroke said.

"Whether it is or not, Gaveston shall not linger here," Mortimer Senior said.

Everyone except King Edward II exited.

"How fast they run to banish him whom I love!" he said. "They would not act if it were something to do me good.

"Why should a King be subject to a priest?

"Proud Rome, which hatches such imperious grooms — servants — with these thy superstitious taper-candles for church rites and prayers, with which thy antichristian churches blaze, I'll burn thy unsound buildings, and force the papal towers to fall and kiss the lowly ground. With slaughtered priests I'll make the Tiber River's channel swell, and raise banks higher with their sepulchers!

"As for the peers who back the clergy thus, if I am King, not one of them shall live."

Gaveston entered the scene and said, "My Lord, I hear it whispered everywhere that I am banished and must flee the land."

"It is true, sweet Gaveston," King Edward II said. "Oh, I wish it were false! The representative of the Pope will have it so, and thou must go away from here, or I shall be deposed.

"But I will reign to be revenged on them, and therefore, sweet friend, take it patiently. Live where thou will, I'll send thee gold enough. And long thou shall not stay in exile; or, if thou do, I'll come to thee. My love shall never turn away from you."

"Is all my hope turned to this Hell of grief?" Gaveston asked.

"Don't tear my heart with thy too piercing words," King Edward II said. "Thou from this land, and I from myself am banished."

Gaveston was King Edward II's other self, and so when Gaveston was banished, the King was banished.

Gaveston said, "To go from here grieves not poor Gaveston, but it grieves him to forsake you, in whose gracious looks the blessedness and supreme happiness of Gaveston remains. For nowhere else does he seek felicity and happiness."

King Edward II said, "And only this torments my wretched soul — that, whether or not I will it, thou must depart.

"Be Governor of Ireland in my stead, and there abide until fortune calls thee home.

"Here, take my picture, and let me wear thine."

They exchanged pictures, and the King said, "Oh, if I might keep thee here, as I do this picture, I would be happy, but now I am most miserable."

"It is something to be pitied by a King," Gaveston said.

"Thou shall not go away from here," King Edward II said. "I'll hide thee, Gaveston."

"If you do, I shall be found, and then I will be hurt more," Gaveston said.

"Kind words and mutual talk make our grief greater," King Edward II said. "Therefore, with silent embracement, let us part."

They hugged, and Gaveston started to leave.

"Wait, Gaveston! I cannot leave thee like this!"

"For every look, my love drops down a tear," Gaveston said. "Seeing I must go, do not renew my sorrow."

"The time is little that thou has left to stay," King Edward II said, "and, therefore, give me leave to look my fill. But, come, sweet friend; I'll accompany thee on thy way."

"The peers will frown," Gaveston said.

"I don't care about their anger," King Edward II said. "Come, let's go. Oh, that we might as well return as go!"

Queen Isabella entered the scene. Accompanying her was Edmund, Earl of Kent, who would say nothing but would closely observe what happened.

"Where is my lord going?" Queen Isabella asked.

"Fawn not on me, French whore," King Edward II, her husband, replied. "Get thee gone."

"On whom but on my husband should I fawn?"

"On Young Mortimer," Gaveston said, "with whom, ungentle Queen …."

He then said to the King, "I say no more. You judge the rest, my lord."

Rumors were circulating that Queen Isabella and Young Mortimer were having an affair.

"In saying this, thou wrong me, Gaveston," Queen Isabella said. "Isn't it enough that thou corrupt my lord, and are a pander to his desires and passions, but thou must call my honor thus in question?"

"I mean not so," Gaveston said. "Your grace must pardon me."

"Thou are too familiar with that Young Mortimer," King Edward II said, "and by thy means Gaveston has been exiled, but I would wish thee to reconcile the lords and get them to agree that Gaveston should stay in England, or thou shall never be reconciled to me."

"Your highness knows that it lies not in my power," Queen Isabella said.

"Go away, then!" King Edward II said. "Don't touch me!"

He then said, "Come, Gaveston."

Queen Isabella said to Gaveston, "Villain, it is thou who rob me of my lord."

"Madam, it is you who rob me of my lord by forcing me to go into exile," Gaveston replied.

"Don't speak to her," King Edward II said. "Let her droop and pine. Let her waste away with suffering."

"My lord, what have I done to deserve these words?" Queen Isabella said. "Witness the tears that Isabella sheds, witness this heart, that, sighing for thee, breaks. How dear my lord is to poor Isabel!"

King Edward II replied, "And may Heaven witness how dear thou are to me."

King Edward II hugged Gaveston.

He added, "There weep, for until the order of exile for my Gaveston is repealed, assure thyself that thou will not come in my sight."

King Edward II and Gaveston exited.

Queen Isabella said to herself, "Oh, miserable and distressed Queen! I wish, when I left sweet France, and was embarked, that charming Circe, walking on the waves, had changed my shape."

In Homer's *Odyssey*, the enchantress Circe changes the shapes of Odysseus' men by turning them into swine. Because she charms men with spells and charms, she is literally charming. In Ovid's *Metamorphoses*, Book 14, Circe walks on waves.

Queen Isabella added, "Or I wish that on my marriage day the cup of Hymen had been full of poison."

Hymen is the god of marriage, and the cup of Hymen refers to a wedding toast.

She continued, "Or I wish that with those — Edward's — arms, which twined about my neck, I had been stifled, and I had not lived to see the King my lord thus to abandon me!

"Like frantic Juno I will fill the earth with ghastly murmur of my sighs and cries. For Jove never doted on Ganymede as much as my husband dotes on cursed Gaveston."

Juno's husband was Jupiter, aka Jove, who was charmed by the beauty of the young Trojan boy Ganymede. Jupiter assumed the form of an eagle and carried Ganymede away to Mount Olympus to be his cupbearer. Juno regarded Ganymede as a romantic rival for Jupiter's love and filled the earth with cries of mourning.

"But that will more aggravate my husband's wrath," Queen Isabella said. "I must plead with him, I must speak fairly to him, and I must be a means to call Gaveston home. And yet my husband will always dote on Gaveston, and so I am miserable forever."

The Earl of Lancaster, the Earl of Warwick, the Earl of Pembroke, Mortimer Senior, and Young Mortimer entered the scene.

"Look where the sister of the King of France sits wringing her hands and beating her breast!" the Earl of Lancaster said.

"The King, I fear, has ill entreated and ill treated her," the Earl of Warwick said.

"Hard is the heart that injures such a saint," the Earl of Pembroke said.

"I know that she weeps because of Gaveston," Young Mortimer said.

"Why?" Mortimer Senior asked. "He is gone."

"Madam, how is your grace?" Young Mortimer asked.

"Ah, Young Mortimer, the King's hate breaks forth now," Queen Isabella said, "and he confesses that he doesn't love me!"

"Cry quittance, madam, then, and don't love him," Young Mortimer said.

To "cry quittance" means 1) to get even, and 2) to renounce your marriage to him.

"No," Queen Isabella said. "Instead, I will die a thousand deaths, and yet I love in vain. He'll never love me."

"Do not fear that, madam," the Earl of Lancaster said. "Now that the King's minion is gone, his wanton humor — amorous disposition — will quickly leave him."

"Oh, never, Lancaster!" Queen Isabella said. "I am forced by him to beg you all for the repeal of his exile. This my lord and husband commands, and this I must perform, or else be banished from his highness' presence."

"You must beg for Gaveston's recall to England?" the Earl of Lancaster said. "Madam! He does not come back, unless the sea vomits up his shipwrecked body."

"And to behold so sweet a sight as that," the Earl of Warwick said, "there's none here who wouldn't run his horse to death in getting to the seashore."

"But, madam, would you have us recall Gaveston home to England?" Young Mortimer asked.

"Aye, Mortimer," Queen Isabella said, "for until Gaveston is restored to England, the angry King has banished me from the court, and, therefore, as thou love and care for me, be my advocate to these peers who are here with you."

"What! Would you have me plead for Gaveston's return out of exile?" Young Mortimer asked.

"Plead for Gaveston whoever will, I am resolved that he shall remain in exile," Mortimer Senior said.

"And so am I, my lord," the Earl of Lancaster said. "Dissuade the Queen."

"Oh, Lancaster, let Mortimer Senior dissuade the King from wanting Gaveston to return," Queen Isabella said, "for it is against my will that Gaveston should return."

"Then don't speak for the King," the Earl of Warwick said. "Let the peasant Gaveston go. Let him stay in exile."

"It is for myself I speak, and not for him," Queen Isabella said.

Although she would argue for Gaveston to return out of exile, she was doing that for herself — to get the King to like her again.

"No speaking in behalf of Gaveston's return to England will prevail with us or avail you," the Earl of Pembroke said, "and therefore cease to argue for his return."

"Fair Queen, forbear to angle for the fish, which being caught, strikes dead him who takes it," Young Mortimer said. "I mean that vile torpedo, Gaveston, who now, I hope, floats on the Irish seas."

A torpedo is an electric ray. It shocks its prey and its enemies.

"Sweet Young Mortimer, sit down by me for a while, and I will tell thee reasons of such weight and importance that thou will soon agree to Gaveston's recall to England," Queen Isabella said.

"That is impossible, but speak your mind," Young Mortimer said.

"And so I will, but none shall hear it but ourselves," Queen Isabella said.

They walked a little distance away and talked quietly together.

"My lords, if the Queen wins Mortimer over to her side, will you be resolute and hold with me?" the Earl of Lancaster asked.

"Not I, against my nephew," Mortimer Senior said.

"Fear not," the Earl of Pembroke said. "The Queen's words cannot alter him."

"No?" the Earl of Warwick said. "See how earnestly she pleads to him!"

"And see how coldly his looks show that he refuses to be persuaded by her words!" the Earl of Lancaster said.

"She smiles," the Earl of Warwick said. "Now, on my life, she has changed his mind!"

"I'll rather lose his friendship, I, than agree that Gaveston shall return to England," the Earl of Lancaster said.

Young Mortimer and Queen Isabella walked over to the nobles.

"Well, of necessity it must be so," Young Mortimer said to Queen Isabella.

He then said, "My lords, that I abhor base Gaveston I hope your honors do not question, and therefore, although I plead for his recall to England, it is not for his sake, but for our advantage. Nay, for the realm's benefit, and for the King's."

"For shame, Young Mortimer, don't dishonor thyself!" the Earl of Lancaster said. "Can this be true, it was good to banish him? And is this also true, it is good to recall him home again? Such reasons make white black, and dark night day."

"My lord of Lancaster, consider the special circumstances," Young Mortimer said.

"In no respect can contraries be true," the Earl of Lancaster said. "One statement and its opposite cannot both be true."

"Yet, my good lord, hear what he can argue," Queen Isabella said.

"All that he speaks is nothing," the Earl of Warwick said. "We are resolved that Gaveston will stay in exile."

"Don't you wish that Gaveston were dead?" Young Mortimer asked.

"I wish he were!" the Earl of Pembroke said.

"Why, then, my lord, give me permission to speak," Young Mortimer said.

"But, nephew, do not play the sophister," Mortimer Senior said. "Don't twist words and logic to make a point."

In classical Greece, Sophists taught rhetoric and argumentation. They were criticized, rightly or wrongly, for teaching their students how to make the weaker argument appear to be the stronger and for making fallacious arguments.

"This that I urge comes from a burning zeal to reform the King and do our country good," Young Mortimer said. "Don't you know that Gaveston has a store of gold, which may in Ireland purchase him such friends — soldiers — who will enable him to confront the mightiest of us all? With all that gold, he can buy himself an army. And as long as he shall live and be beloved, it is hard for us to bring about his overthrow."

"He is making a good point, my lord of Lancaster," the Earl of Warwick said.

"But, if he were here, detested as he is," Young Mortimer said, "how easily might some base slave be bribed to greet his lordship with a dagger; and no one would so much as blame the murderer, but rather praise him for that splendid undertaking and in the history books write his name for purging the realm of such a plague!"

"He speaks the truth," the Earl of Pembroke said.

"Yes, but how chances it this was not done before?" the Earl of Lancaster asked.

"Because, my lords, it was not thought upon," Young Mortimer said. "Nay, more, when he shall know it lies in us to banish him, and then to call him home, it will make him vail the top flag of his pride, and fear to offend even the lowest-ranked nobleman."

On the sea a ship sometimes lowered its top flag as a sign of respect to another ship.

"But what if he doesn't, nephew?" Mortimer Senior asked.

"Then we may with some pretext rise up in arms," Young Mortimer said, "for, despite however much we have endured, it is treason to be up against the King. So we shall need to have the people on our side or else the people would overwhelm us members of the nobility. The people lean to the King for his father's sake, but they cannot tolerate such a night-grown mushroom as my lord of Cornwall is. We can, therefore, go up against Gaveston with the people's support."

Mushrooms grow overnight, and so they are a symbol for an upstart, a quickly rising man whom others resent.

He continued, "And, when the common people and the nobles join, not even the King can act as a buckler — a shield — for Gaveston. We'll pull him from the strongest stronghold — castle — he has. My lords, if to perform this I should be slack, think that I am as low a creature as Gaveston."

"On that condition Lancaster will agree," the Earl of Lancaster said.

"And so will Pembroke," the Earl of Pembroke said.

"And I," the Earl of Warwick said.

"And I," Mortimer Senior said.

"In this I count myself highly gratified and pleased, and I, Mortimer, will rest at your command," Young Mortimer said.

"And when this favor Isabel forgets, then let her live abandoned and forlorn," Isabella said. "But see, opportunely, my lord the King, having accompanied Gaveston, the Earl of Cornwall, to his point of departure, has newly returned. This news will much gladden him, yet not as much as me. I love him more than he can love Gaveston. I wish the King loved me only half as much as he loves Gaveston! Then I would be triply blest."

King Edward II, mourning, entered the scene, along with Lord Beaumont, one of his supporters. The Clerk of the Court accompanied them.

King Edward II said, "He's gone, and for his absence thus I mourn. Did never sorrow go so near my heart as does the absence of my sweet Gaveston? And, if my crown's revenue could bring him back, I would freely give it to his enemies, and think I gained, having bought so dear a friend."

"Listen!" Queen Isabella said. "How he harps upon his minion!"

"My heart is like an anvil for sorrow, which beats upon it like the Cyclopes' hammers, and which with the noise upsets my dizzy brain, and makes me frantic for my Gaveston," King Edward II said.

The Cyclopes were one-eyed giants who helped the blacksmith god Vulcan forge Jupiter's lightning bolts with hammers and anvils.

King Edward II continued, "Ah, if only some bloodless Fury had arisen from Hell, and with my kingly scepter struck me dead, when I was forced to leave my Gaveston!"

The Furies were avenging spirits from the Land of the Dead.

"*Diablo!* The Devil!" the Earl of Lancaster said. "What passionate lamentations do you call these?"

"My gracious lord, I come to bring you news," Isabella said.

"That you have negotiated with your Mortimer?" King Edward II asked.

"That Gaveston, my lord, shall be recalled to England," Isabella replied.

"Recalled!" King Edward II said. "The news is too sweet to be true."

"But will you love me, if you find that it is true?" Isabella asked.

"If it is true, what won't Edward do?" King Edward II asked rhetorically.

"For Gaveston, but not for Isabel," the Queen said.

"For thee, fair Queen, if thou love Gaveston, I'll hang a golden tongue about thy neck, seeing thou have pleaded with so good success," King Edward II said.

A golden tongue is a piece of jewelry: a pendant in the form of a tongue — for example, a serpent's tongue decorated with gems.

He hugged and kissed her.

"Hang no other jewels around my neck than these arms of yours, my lord," Queen Isabella said, "nor let me have more wealth than I may fetch from this rich treasury that is your mouth. Oh, how a kiss revives poor Isabel!"

"Once more take my hand," King Edward II said, "and let this be a second marriage between thyself and me."

"And may it prove happier than the first!" Queen Isabella said. "My gentle lord, speak in a friendly way to these nobles who wait in attendance for a gracious look and on their knees salute your majesty."

"Courageous Lancaster, embrace thy King," King Edward II said, "and, as thick mists perish by the Sun, even so let hatred perish with thy sovereign's smile. Live thou with me as my companion."

"This salutation overjoys my heart," the Earl of Lancaster said.

"Warwick shall be my chiefest counselor," King Edward II said. "These silver hairs of his will adorn my court more than extravagant silks or rich embroidery. Chide me, sweet Warwick, if I go astray."

"Slay me, my lord, when I offend your grace," the Earl of Warwick replied.

"In solemn processions and in public entertainments, Pembroke shall bear the sword of state before the King," Edward II said.

"And with this sword Pembroke will fight for you," the Earl of Pembroke said.

"But why does Young Mortimer walk apart from the others?" King Edward II said. "Be thou commander of our royal fleet, or if that lofty office does not please thee, I make thee here Lord Marshal of the realm."

The Lord Marshall was the commander of the King's armies.

"My lord, I'll marshal so your enemies," Young Mortimer said, "that England shall be quiet, and you safe."

"And as for you, Mortimer Senior, Lord of Chirk, whose great achievements in our foreign war deserve no common place nor mean reward, you shall be the general of the levied troops who now are ready to assail the Scots," King Edward II said.

Chirk is in Wales, just across the border from England.

"In this your grace has highly honored me," Mortimer Senior said, "for with my nature war does best agree."

"Now is the King of England rich and strong because he has the love of his renowned peers," Queen Isabella said.

King Edward II said, "Yes, Isabel, never was my heart so light and carefree.

"Clerk of the Crown, to Ireland direct our warrant for Gaveston to return to England!"

The Clerk of the Crown would write the warrant for Gaveston to return out of exile.

"Beaumont, fly — go quickly — to Ireland as fast as Iris or Jove's Mercury."

Beaumont would carry the warrant to Ireland and give it to Gaveston.

Iris and Mercury were the as-fast-as-the-wind messengers of the gods.

"It shall be done, my gracious lord," Beaumont said.

Beaumont and the Clerk of the Court exited.

King Edward II said, "Lord Mortimer Senior, we leave you to your duty.

"Now let us go in, and feast royally in anticipation of the coming of our friend Gaveston, the Earl of Cornwall.

"We'll have a general jousting contest and tournament, and then his marriage shall be solemnized; for don't you know that I have engaged him to be married to Lady Margaret de Clare, our niece and the Earl of Gloucester's heir?"

"Such news we hear, my lord," the Earl of Lancaster said.

"On that day, if not for him, yet for my sake — I who in the tournament will be the challenger and dare all comers to fight me — spare no cost," King Edward II said. "We will requite your love."

"In this or in anything your highness shall command us," the Earl of Warwick said.

"Thanks, gentle Warwick," King Edward II said. "Come, let's go in and revel."

Everyone except the Mortimers exited.

"Nephew, I must go to Scotland," Mortimer Senior said. "Thou will stay here. Cease now to oppose thyself against the King. Thou see that he is mild and calm by nature. And seeing his mind so dotes on Gaveston, let him without restraint have his will and do what he wants.

"The mightiest Kings have had their minions. Alexander the Great loved his lifelong friend Hephaestion. The conquering Hercules wept for Hylas, and stern Achilles languished for Patroclus."

When Hephaestion died suddenly, Alexander the Great mourned for him. When Hylas went missing, Hercules wept for him. In the Trojan War, Achilles' friend Patroclus was killed in battle, leading Achilles to mourn excessively.

Mortimer Senior continued:

"And not Kings only, but the wisest men. The Roman orator Marcus Tullius Cicero loved Octavius, who became Caesar Augustus, and the grave

Greek philosopher Socrates loved the wild and beautiful Athenian politician and general Alcibiades.

"So then let his grace the King, whose youth is flexible and promises as much as we can wish, freely enjoy without constraint that vain lightheaded Gaveston, Earl of Cornwall. For riper years will wean him from such trifles. When he is older and more mature, he will reject Gaveston."

"Uncle, the King's wanton character and inclinations do not grieve me. But this I scorn, that one as basely born as Gaveston should by his sovereign's favor grow so impertinent, and engage in riotous living by spending the treasury of the realm, while soldiers mutiny for lack of pay.

"He wears clothing worth a lord's revenue in rents on his back, and, like Midas, for whom everything he touched turned to gold, Gaveston struts in the court, with base foreign rogues at his heels, whose proud fantastic outfits make such show as if Proteus, god of shapes, appeared."

Proteus, a god known as the Old Man of the Sea, could change shapes, as he does in Homer's *Odyssey* when Menelaus, King of Sparta, and some of his men capture him and hold on tight until he stops shape-shifting and agrees to tell Menelaus what will happen in the future.

Young Mortimer continued, "I have not seen a dapper jack so brisk. He wears a short Italian hooded cloak, extravagantly decorated with pearl, and in his fashionable cap from Tuscany he wears a jewel of more value than the crown. While others walk below, the King and he, from out a window, laugh at such as we, and mock our train of attendants, and jest at our attire.

"Uncle, it is this that makes me angry."

"But, nephew, now you see that the King has changed," Mortimer Senior said.

"Then so have I, and I live to do him service," Young Mortimer said. "But, while I have a sword, a hand, and a heart, I will not yield to any such upstart. You know my mind. Come, uncle, let's leave."

CHAPTER 2
— 2.1 —
[Scene 5]

Young Spenser and Baldock talked together. Young Spenser was Lady Margaret de Clare's attendant, and Baldock was her tutor. Now that their employer, the Earl of Gloucester, had died, they were deciding whom to serve. This involved deciding who would be able to do them the most good.

"Young Spenser, seeing that our lord, the Earl of Gloucester, is dead, which of the nobles do thou mean to serve?" Baldock asked.

"Not Young Mortimer, nor any of his side, because the King and he are enemies," Young Spenser replied. "Baldock, learn this from me: A factious, seditious lord shall hardly do himself good, much less us, but he who has the favor of a King may with one word advance us in our careers while we live. Therefore, the liberal Gaveston, Earl of Cornwall, is the man on whose good fortune Spenser's hope depends."

The word "liberal" can mean 1) generous, 2) gentleman-like, and 3) licentious.

"Do you intend, then, to be his retainer?" Baldock asked.

"No, his companion, for he loves me well," Young Spenser said, "and he would have once recommended me to the King."

"But Gaveston is banished," Baldock said. "There's small hope of advancement coming from him."

"Yes, he is banished for a while," Young Spenser said, "but, Baldock, just see what will happen. A friend of mine told me in secrecy that Gaveston's exile has been repealed and he has been sent for to return to England again. And just now a post came from the court with letters to our Lady Margaret de Clare from the King. And, as she read, she smiled, which makes me think she was reading about her lover, Gaveston."

"It is likely enough," Baldock said, "for, since he was exiled, she neither walks abroad nor comes within the sight of most people. But I had thought the match had been broken off, and that his banishment had changed her mind."

"Our lady's first love is not wavering," Young Spenser said. "I'll bet my life against thine that she will marry Gaveston."

"Our lady" is the woman whom they had been serving: Lady Margaret de Clare, the sister of the Earl of Gloucester and the niece of King Edward II.

"Then I hope by her means to be advanced in rank, having been tutor to her since she was a child," Baldock said.

"Then, Baldock, you must cease to behave like a scholar, and learn to court it like a gentleman," Young Spenser said. "It is not a black coat and a little neckband, a velvet caped cloak, trimmed with an overlay of coarse serge cloth, and smelling a bouquet of flowers all the day, or holding a handkerchief in your hand, or saying a long grace at a table's end" — the bottom of the table was for the guests with the lowest social standing. Salt was at the other end of the table for the use of the more important guests — "or making deep bows to a nobleman, or looking downward, with your eyelids closed in deep modesty, and saying, 'Truly, if it may please your honor,' that can get you any favor with great men.

"Instead, you must be proud, bold, jocular, and resolute, and now and then stab someone, as occasion serves."

This kind of "stab" could be sexual, or it could be a betrayal or a biting remark, or it could be a figurative or literal stab in the back.

In other words, according to Young Spenser, if you want to get ahead in life, don't be a scholar; instead, be proud at court and occasionally a lover or backstabber. But perhaps he was joking with his friend.

"Young Spenser, thou know I hate such trifling conventions of dress and behavior, and engage in them only out of complete hypocrisy," Baldock said.

This may sound as if he is rejecting conventions of dress and behavior for attendants at court, but his next words make it clear that he is rejecting conventions of dress and behavior for scholars.

Baldock continued:

"My former lord, the Earl of Gloucester, while he lived, was so puritanical that he would take exceptions at my buttons and even when they were like pins' heads, he would blame me for their bigness, which made me curate-like in my attire, although I was inwardly licentious enough, and ready for any kind of villainy.

"I am none of these common, ordinary pedants, I, who cannot speak without *propterea quod*."

"*Propterea quod*" is Latin for "because of this." Baldock was saying that he is not like a common, ordinary pedantic scholar because he always used phrases such as "*propterea quod*" and reasoned correctly.

"But you are one of those who say '*quandoquidem*,' and you have a special gift to form a verb," Young Spenser said.

"*Quandoquidem*" is Latin for "inasmuch." Young Spenser was teasing Baldock by implying that he was more like a common, ordinary pedantic scholar than he thought. The use of fancy words does not necessarily mean that the person using them is reasoning correctly.

"To form a verb" meant "to make a nice turn of phrase" or, perhaps, "to conjugate a verb." Again, Young Spenser was teasing Baldock.

"Leave off this jesting," Baldock said. "Here comes my lady."

Lady Margaret de Clare entered the room.

Not seeing Baldock and Young Spenser, she looked at a letter and said to herself, "The grief for his exile was not as great as is the joy of his returning home. This letter came from my sweet Gaveston. What need thou, love, thus to excuse thyself? I know thou could not come and visit me."

She read out loud, "*I will not long be from thee though I die.*"

"This proves the entire love of my lord," she said.

She read out loud, "*When I forsake thee, may death seize on my heart.*"

"But rest thee here where Gaveston shall sleep," she said.

She put the letter in her bosom.

Looking at another letter, she said, "Now to the letter of my lord the King. He wants me to go to the court, and meet my Gaveston. Why do I hesitate, seeing that he talks thus of my marriage day?"

She called for an attendant: "Who's there?"

Seeing Baldock, she said, "Baldock! See that my coach is made ready. I must go away from here."

"It shall be done, madam," Baldock said.

"And meet me at the park pale — the park fence — directly," Lady Margaret de Clare ordered.

Baldock exited.

She then said, "Spenser, stay and keep me company, for I have joyful news to tell thee. My lord of Cornwall is coming over from Ireland to England, and he will be at the court as soon as we."

"I knew the King would have him home again," Young Spenser said.

"If all things work out as I hope they will," she said, "thy service, Spenser, shall be thought upon and remembered."

In other words, he would receive a reward.

"I humbly thank your ladyship," Young Spenser said.

"Come lead the way. I am restless until I am there," Lady Margaret de Clare said.

— 2.2 —

[Scene 6]

King Edward II, Queen Isabella, the Earl of Lancaster, Young Mortimer, the Earl of Warwick, the Earl of Pembroke, the Earl of Kent, and some attendants were before the castle at Tynemouth on the coast in northern England, awaiting the return of Gaveston.

"The wind is good. I wonder why he is delayed. I fear that he is shipwrecked upon the sea," King Edward II said.

"Look, Lancaster, how wracked by sorrow he is, and always his mind thinks about his minion," Queen Isabella said quietly to the Earl of Lancaster.

"My lord," the Earl of Lancaster said.

"What is it? What is the news? Has Gaveston arrived?" King Edward II asked.

"Nothing but Gaveston!" Young Mortimer said. "What means your grace? You have matters of more weight to think upon. The King of France sets foot in Normandy."

England and France were battling for control of this province.

"A trifle!" King Edward II said. "We'll expel him when we please. But tell me, Mortimer, what's thy device you made in preparation for use in the stately tournament we decreed?"

A device is a heraldic emblem — design and motto — on a shield. King Edward II had ordered the nobles to each make a device for the upcoming tournament.

"A modest one, my lord, not worth the telling," Young Mortimer said.

"Please let me know it," the King said.

"But seeing you're so desirous," Young Mortimer said, "thus it is: A lofty cedar tree fair flourishing, on whose top branches kingly eagles perch, and by the bark a cankerworm creeps up, and gets to the highest bough of all. The motto: *Aeque tandem*."

The cankerworm is a parasite, which here represents Gaveston ambitiously climbing up the social ladder. The Latin motto "*Aeque tandem*" means "Equal at last."

"And what is yours, my lord of Lancaster?" King Edward II asked.

"My lord, mine's more obscure than Young Mortimer's," the Earl of Lancaster said. "The Roman scholar Pliny reports that there is a flying fish that all the other fishes deadly hate, and therefore when being pursued, it takes to the air. No sooner is it up, but there's a fowl that seizes it: This fish, my lord, I bear. The motto is this: *Undique mors est.*"

The flying fish represents, of course, Gaveston, and the design and the motto present what the nobles have planned for him. The Latin motto "*Undique mors est*" means "Death is everywhere."

"Proud Mortimer, ungentle Lancaster, is this the love you bear your sovereign?" King Edward II said. "Is this the fruit your reconciliation bears? Can you with words make a show of amity, and yet in your shields display your rancorous minds that are filled with ill will? What call you this but private defamation against Gaveston, who is both the Earl of Cornwall and my figurative brother?"

"Sweet husband, be content," Queen Isabella said. "They all love you."

"Who hates my Gaveston does not love me," King Edward II said. "I am that cedar; don't shake me too much. And you are the eagles. No matter how high you soar, I have the jesses that will pull you down."

A "jess" is a strap attached to the leg of a hawk.

He continued, "And *aeque tandem* shall that cankerworm cry to the proudest peer of Britain."

King Edward II meant that even the proudest English nobleman would know that Gaveston was his equal.

He continued, "Though thou compare him to a flying fish, and threaten death whether he rise or fall, it is not the hugest monster of the sea nor the foulest Harpy that shall swallow him."

Harpies were mythological half-woman, half-bird creatures that would rush on food, eat some of it, and render the rest unsuitable for consumption. In Virgil's *Aeneid*, Harpies harass Aeneas and his men. In Apollonius of Rhodes' *Argonautica*, Harpies harass King Phineus of Thrace.

"If in Gaveston's absence the King favors him like this, what will he do when Gaveston shall be present?" Young Mortimer said quietly to the Earl of Lancaster.

"That we shall see," the Earl of Lancaster replied. "Look! His lordship is coming!"

Gaveston arrived.

"My Gaveston!" King Edward II said. "Welcome to Tynemouth! Welcome to thy friend!"

In this culture, the word "friend" could mean "lover."

He continued, "Thy absence made me languish and waste away. Just as the lovers of fair Danaë, when she was locked up in a bronze tower, desired her more, and grew wild, so also do I."

Danaë's father, King Acrisius of Argos, heard a prophecy that Danaë's son would grow up and kill him, so he locked her in a tower. Zeus, King of the gods, saw her, lusted after her, and visited her after taking the form of a shower of gold. Danaë then gave birth to Perseus, who grew up and accidentally killed her father, King Acrisius of Argos.

King Edward II continued, "And now thy sight is sweeter far than thy parting from here was bitter and irksome to my sobbing heart."

"Sweet lord and King, your speech anticipates mine," Gaveston said, "yet I have words left to express my joy. The shepherd, nipped with biting winter's rage, frolics not more to see the colorful-with-flowers spring than I do to behold your majesty."

"Will none of you salute my Gaveston?" King Edward II asked the nobles.

"Salute him?" the Earl of Lancaster said. "Yes. Welcome, Lord Chamberlain!"

"Welcome is the good Earl of Cornwall!" Young Mortimer said.

"Welcome, Lord Governor of the Isle of Man!" the Earl of Warwick said.

"Welcome, master Secretary!" the Earl of Pembroke said.

Earlier, King Edward II had made Gaveston Lord High Chamberlain, Chief Secretary to the State and King, Earl of Cornwall, and King and Lord of Man.

The tone of the nobles' voices showed that they were insincere in their welcomes.

"Brother, do you hear them?" the Earl of Kent asked the King.

"Will these Earls and Barons always treat me like this?" King Edward II complained.

"My lord, I cannot endure these injuries," Gaveston said.

"Ah, me, poor soul, when these begin to quarrel!" Queen Isabella said.

"Reject their abuse and return it to their throats," King Edward II said to Gaveston. "I'll be thy protection."

"Base, leaden Earls, who glory in your birth," Gaveston said, "go sit at home, and eat your tenants' beef."

At the time, Frenchmen such as Gaveston regarded the English as eating lots of beef that rendered them slow-witted, aka beef-witted.

Gaveston continued, "Don't come here to scoff at Gaveston, whose soaring thoughts did never creep so low as to bestow a look on such as you."

"Yet I disdain not to do this for you," the Earl of Lancaster said, drawing his sword.

King Edward II saw the sword and cried, "Treason! Treason!"

To draw a sword in the presence of the King was a serious offense.

In the turmoil that followed, he shouted, "Where's the traitor?"

The Earl of Pembroke pointed at Gaveston and said, "Here! Here!"

"Take Gaveston away from here," King Edward II said. "They'll murder him."

"The life of thee shall pay for this foul disgrace," Gaveston said to the Earl of Lancaster.

"Villain, thy life shall pay unless I miss my aim," Young Mortimer said.

Young Mortimer wounded Gaveston.

"Ah, furious Mortimer, what have thou done?" Queen Isabella asked.

"No more than I would answer — publicly justify — if he were slain," he replied.

Gaveston exited with some attendants.

King Edward II said to Young Mortimer, "Yes, more than thou can answer — atone for — though Gaveston live. Dearly shall both you and the Earl of Lancaster abide — pay for — this riotous deed. Get out of my presence! Don't come near the court."

"I'll not be barred from the court on account of Gaveston," Young Mortimer said.

"We'll drag him by the ears to the block so he can be beheaded," the Earl of Lancaster said.

"Look after your own heads," King Edward II said. "Gaveston's head is safe enough."

"Look after your own crown, if you back Gaveston like this," the Earl of Warwick said.

The crown could be the crown the King wore on his head, or it could be the crown of the King's own head.

"Warwick, these words do ill beseem thy years," the Earl of Kent said. "You are old enough to speak wiser words."

"All of them conspire to cross and obstruct me thus," King Edward II said, "but if I live, I'll tread upon the heads of those who think with high looks thus to tread me down."

He added, "Come, Edmund, let's go away, and levy men to raise an army. It is war that must abate these Barons' pride."

King Edward II, Queen Isabella, and Edmund, Earl of Kent, exited.

"Let's go to our castles, for the King is moved," the Earl of Warwick said.

"Moved may he be, and perish in his wrath!" Young Mortimer said.

"Moved" can mean "angry," but it can also mean "Moved from the throne."

"Cousin, there is no dealing with him now," the Earl of Lancaster said to Young Mortimer.

The word "cousin" was used in this culture to refer to many kinds of biological relationships and even to close friends.

He added, "He means to make us bow down and submit to him by force of arms. Therefore, let us here jointly vow to pursue that Gaveston to the death."

"By Heaven, the contemptible villain shall not live!" Young Mortimer said.

"I'll have his blood, or die in seeking it," the Earl of Warwick said.

"The like oath Pembroke takes," the Earl of Pembroke said.

"And so does Lancaster," the Earl of Lancaster said. "Now send our heralds to defy and renounce allegiance to the King, and make the people swear to put him down."

A messenger carrying letters arrived.

"Letters?" Young Mortimer said. "From where?"

"From Scotland, my lord," the messenger replied.

Young Mortimer began reading the letters.

"Why, how is it now, cousin? How fare all our friends?" the Earl of Lancaster asked.

"My uncle's been taken prisoner by the Scots," Young Mortimer said.

"We'll have him ransomed, man," the Earl of Lancaster said. "Be of good cheer."

High-ranking prisoners were often ransomed for large amounts of money.

"They rate his ransom at five thousand pounds," Young Mortimer said. "Who should pay the money but the King, seeing that my uncle has been taken prisoner in his wars? I'll go to the King."

"Do, cousin, and I'll accompany thee," the Earl of Lancaster said.

"In the meantime, my lord of Pembroke and I myself will go to Newcastle here, and raise forces," the Earl of Warwick said.

"Go about it, then, and we will follow you," Young Mortimer said.

"Be resolute and determined and full of secrecy," the Earl of Lancaster advised.

"I promise you that I will," the Earl of Warwick said.

Everyone except Young Mortimer and the Earl of Lancaster exited.

Young Mortimer and the Earl of Lancaster went to see King Edward II.

"Cousin, if he will not ransom him," Young Mortimer said, "I'll thunder such a peal of words into his ears as a subject never did to his King."

"Good," the Earl of Lancaster said. "I'll bear my part."

He called, "Holla, who's there?"

A guard entered.

"Yes, indeed, such a guard as this does well," Young Mortimer said.

Young Mortimer could guess that the guard's purpose was to keep him away from the King.

"Lead on the way," the Earl of Lancaster said.

The guard asked, "Where do your lordships wish to go?"

"Where else but to the King?" Young Mortimer said.

"His highness is disposed to be alone," the guard said.

"Why, he may be disposed to be alone," the Earl of Lancaster said, "but we will speak to him."

"You may not go in to see the King, my lord," the guard replied.

"May we not?" Young Mortimer said.

King Edward II and the Earl of Kent arrived.

"What's going on now?" the King asked. "What noise is this? Who have we there? Is it you?"

He started to leave.

"Wait, my lord," Young Mortimer said. "I come to bring you news. My uncle's been taken prisoner by the Scots."

"Then ransom him," King Edward II said.

"He was taken prisoner while fighting for you in your wars," the Earl of Lancaster said. "You should ransom him."

"And you shall ransom him, or else ...," Young Mortimer said.

"What, Mortimer! You will not threaten him?" the Earl of Kent said.

"Quiet yourself," King Edward II said to Young Mortimer. "You shall have the broad seal — letters patent — allowing you to gather money for him throughout the realm."

The King meant that Young Mortimer would have an official document that allowed him to travel through England and raise money for the ransom of his uncle without being penalized for begging. This was an insult because it implied that Young Mortimer was impoverished and unable to pay the ransom himself. In addition, it made it clear that the King would not pay the ransom out of the royal treasury.

"Your minion Gaveston has taught you to treat us this way," the Earl of Lancaster said.

"My lord, the family of the Mortimers is not so poor," Young Mortimer said. "If they were to sell their land, the money raised would levy men enough to anger you."

The men levied would form an army.

Young Mortimer added, "We never beg, but instead use such prayers as these."

He put his hand on the hilt of his sword.

"Shall I always be haunted and tormented like this!" King Edward II said.

"Now that you are here alone, I'll speak my mind," Young Mortimer said to King Edward II.

"And so will I," the Earl of Lancaster said, "and then, my lord, farewell."

"The foolish triumphs, masques, lascivious shows, and prodigal, extravagant gifts bestowed on Gaveston have drained thy treasure dry, and made thee weak," Young Mortimer said. "The discontented common people break."

Apparently, the common people were discontented and almost to the breaking point because of high taxes.

"Look for rebellion," the Earl of Lancaster said. "Look to be deposed. Thy garrisons are beaten out of France, and lame and poor, they lie groaning at the gates. The wild Ulster clan chieftain O'Neill, with swarms of Irish kerns — foot-soldiers — lives uncontrolled within the English pale."

The English pale consisted of the regions of Ireland around Dublin where English settlers lived. This area was safer for English settlers than other parts of Ireland.

He continued, "To the walls of York, the Scots make raids, and, unresisted, draw away rich spoils."

"The arrogant Dane commands the narrow seas, while in the harbor ride at anchor thy ships unrigged," Young Mortimer said.

The narrow seas are the English Channel.

"What foreign Prince sends ambassadors to thee?" the Earl of Lancaster asked.

"Who loves thee, but a crew of flatterers?" Young Mortimer asked.

"Thy gentle Queen, sole sister to Valois, complains that thou has left her all forlorn and abandoned," the Earl of Lancaster said.

Queen Isabella was French. She was King Philip IV of France's sole daughter, and she had three brothers who became Kings of France: Charles IV, Philip V, and Louis X. They were actually of the House of Capet; the House of Valois was a related house. Queen Isabella's cousin, Philip of Valois, became King Philip VI of France, succeeding Charles IV.

"Thy court is naked, being emptied of those who make a King appear glorious to the world — I mean the peers, whom thou should dearly love," Young Mortimer said. "Subversive leaflets and pamphlets are cast against thee in the street. Ballads and rhymes are made about thy overthrow."

The Earl of Lancaster said, "English citizens living on the northern borders by Scotland, seeing their houses burned and their wives and children slain by Scottish raiders, run up and down, cursing the name of thee and Gaveston."

"When were thou in the field of battle with your military banners spread?" Young Mortimer said. "Only once, and then thy soldiers marched like stage actors, with garish robes, not armor. And thou thyself, decorated with gold, rode laughing at the rest, nodding and shaking the sparkling crest of your helmet, where women's favors — tokens of affection — hung down like ribbons."

"And because of that military campaign, the mocking, sneering Scots, to England's high disgrace, have made this jig, this insulting piece of doggerel:

"*Maids of England, sore may you mourn,*

"*For your lemans [sweethearts] you have lost at Bannockburn,*

"*With a heave and a ho!*

"*What weeneth [hopes] the King of England*

"*So soon to have won Scotland?*

"*With a rumbelow!*"

The word "rumbelow" was a nonsense word used in ballads.

On 24 June 1314, in the Battle of Bannockburn, King Robert Bruce of Scotland defeated an army led by King Edward II of England.

"Wigmore Castle shall fly to set my uncle free," Young Mortimer said.

Young Mortimer had a castle at Wigmore; he intended to sell it to raise money to free his uncle.

"And, when it is gone, our swords shall purchase — acquire — more," the Earl of Lancaster said. "If you — King Edward II and the Earl of Kent — are angry, revenge it as you can. Look next to see us with our battle standards spread."

Young Mortimer and the Earl of Lancaster exited.

"My swelling heart breaks from anger," King Edward II said. "How often have I been baited by these peers, and dare not be revenged, for their power is great. Yet shall the crowing of these young cocks frighten a lion? Edward, unfold thy paws, and let their lives' blood slake thy fury's hunger. If I be cruel and grow tyrannous, now let them thank themselves, and regret it too late."

"My lord, I see your love to Gaveston will be the ruin of the realm and you, for now the wrathful nobles threaten wars," the Earl of Kent said. "So therefore, brother, banish him forever."

"Are thou an enemy to my Gaveston?" King Edward II asked.

"Yes, and it grieves me that I favored him," the Earl of Kent said.

"Traitor, be gone!" King Edward II said. "Whine with Mortimer."

"So I will, rather than with Gaveston," the Earl of Kent said.

"Get out of my sight, and trouble me no more!" King Edward II said.

"It is no wonder, though, that thou scorn thy noble peers, when I thy brother am rejected like this," the Earl of Kent said.

He exited.

"Go!" King Edward II said. "Poor Gaveston, thou have no friend but me. Do what they can, we'll live in Tynemouth Castle here, and as long as I walk with him about the walls, what do I care, although the Earls surround us?

"Here comes the woman who is the cause of all these quarrels."

Queen Isabella, Lady Margaret de Clare, and two ladies-in-waiting entered the scene. Gaveston, Baldock, and Young Spenser accompanied them.

"My lord, it is thought the Earls are up in arms and rebelling," Queen Isabella said.

"Yes, and it is likewise thought you favor him," King Edward II said.

Edward II was thinking of Queen Isabella's reputed affair with Young Mortimer.

"Thus you still suspect me without cause," Queen Isabella said.

"Sweet uncle, speak more kindly to the Queen," Lady Margaret de Clare requested.

"My lord, deceive her," Gaveston whispered to King Edward II. "Speak fair, courteous words to her."

"Pardon me, sweet," King Edward II said to his Queen. "I forgot myself."

"Your pardon is quickly gotten from Isabel," she replied.

"The younger Mortimer is grown so defiant that to my face he threatens civil wars," King Edward II said.

"Why don't you commit him to the Tower of London?" Gaveston asked.

"I dare not, for the people well love him," King Edward II said.

"Why, then, we'll have him secretly murdered," Gaveston said.

"I wish that the Earl of Lancaster and he had both drunk a bowl of poison to each other's health!" King Edward II said. "But let's not talk about them. Tell me who are these two men."

He was referring to Young Spenser and Baldock.

"They are two of my father's servants while he lived," Lady Margaret de Clare said. "May it please your grace to employ them now."

"Tell me, where were thou born?" King Edward II asked. "What is thine coat of arms?"

"My name is Baldock, and my rank of gentleman I fetched from Oxford, not from heraldry."

His title of gentleman came from the degree he had earned from Oxford; it was not a hereditary title.

"The fitter are thou, Baldock, for my needs," King Edward II said. "Serve me, and I'll see thou shall not lack what you need."

In fact, Baldock would become King Edward II's Chancellor, aka Secretary.

"I humbly thank your majesty," Baldock replied.

Referring to Young Spenser, King Edward II asked, "Do you know this other man, Gaveston?"

"Yes, my lord," Gaveston answered. "His name is Spenser; he is of a good family. For my sake let him wait upon your grace. Scarcely shall you find a man who is more deserving."

"Then, Spenser, wait upon me," King Edward II said. "For Gaveston's sake I'll grace thee with a higher social status before long."

"No greater social status could befall me than to be favored by your majesty!" Young Spenser replied.

"Margaret, this day shall be your marriage feast," King Edward II said. "And, Gaveston, think that I love thee well to wed thee to our niece, the only heir to the recently deceased Earl of Gloucester."

"I know, my lord, that many will resent me," Gaveston said, "but I respect neither their love nor their hate."

"The headstrong Barons shall not limit me," King Edward II said. "He whom I choose to favor shall be great.

"Come, let's go, and when the marriage ceremony ends, then we will have at — fight — the rebels and their accomplices."

— 2.3 —

[Scene 7]

The Earl of Lancaster, Young Mortimer, the Earl of Warwick, the Earl of Pembroke, and the Earl of Kent talked together.

"My lords, because of our love for this our native land," the Earl of Kent said, "I have come to join with you, and leave the King. And in your quarrel, and for the good of the realm, I will be the first who shall risk my life."

"I fear that you are sent out of deceit as part of a plot to undermine us with a show of love," the Earl of Lancaster said.

"King Edward II is your brother; therefore, we have cause to suspect the worst, and to doubt that you are really revolting against your brother," the Earl of Warwick said.

"My honor shall be the pledge of my truth and honesty," the Earl of Kent said. "If that will not suffice, then farewell, my lords."

"Wait, Edmund," Young Mortimer said, using the Earl of Kent's given name. "Never was a Plantagenet false of his word; and therefore we trust thee."

Actually, King Edward II was a Plantagenet, and the rebelling nobles distrusted him.

The Plantagenet dynasty began with King Henry II in 1154, and ended with King Richard III in 1485.

"But what's the reason you should leave him now?" the Earl of Pembroke asked.

"I have informed the Earl of Lancaster of my reason," the Earl of Kent said.

"And his reason is sufficient," the Earl of Lancaster said. "Now, my lords, know this: Gaveston has secretly arrived, and here in Tynemouth he frolics with the King."

Actually, all the nobles already knew this, and Gaveston's return was not made in secret.

The Earl of Lancaster continued, "Let us with these our followers scale the walls, and suddenly surprise them unawares."

"I'll give the signal and lead the attack," Young Mortimer said.

"And I'll follow thee," the Earl of Warwick said.

"This tattered ensign of my ancestors, which swept the desert shore of that Dead Sea from where we got the name of Mortimer, I will advance upon these castle walls," Young Mortimer said.

According to Young Mortimer, the Mortimer family got its name from an ancestor who was a Crusader and saw the Dead Sea, which is *Mer Mort* in French and *Mortuum Mare* in Latin. Actually, the name came from the village of Mortemer in Normandy.

He continued, "Drummers, strike the alarum — the call to arms — and rouse them from their idle pastimes, and ring aloud the death knell of Gaveston!"

"None be so bold as to touch the King," the Earl of Lancaster said. "But spare neither Gaveston nor his friends."

— 2.4 —

[Scene 8]

King Edward II and Young Spenser talked together in a room of Tynemouth Castle, which was under attack and close to falling.

"Oh, tell me, Young Spenser, where is Gaveston?" King Edward II asked.

"I fear that he has been slain, my gracious lord," Young Spenser replied.

"No, here he comes," King Edward II said. "Now let them plunder and kill."

Gaveston, Queen Isabella, and Lady Margaret de Clare walked over to them.

"Flee, flee, my lords," King Edward II said. "The Earls have captured the stronghold. Board a ship, and flee to Scarborough. Young Spenser and I will ride quickly away by land."

"Oh, stay, my lord," Gaveston said. "They will not injure you."

"I will not trust them, Gaveston!" King Edward II said. "Leave!"

"Farewell, my lord," Gaveston said.

"Lady, farewell," King Edward II said to Lady Margaret de Clare.

"Farewell, sweet uncle, until we meet again," Lady Margaret de Clare replied.

Lady Margaret and her husband, Gaveston, wanted to sail about 70 miles south of Tynemouth to the castle at Scarborough.

"Farewell, sweet Gaveston," King Edward II said, "and farewell, niece."

"No farewell to poor Isabel thy Queen?" Queen Isabella asked.

"Yes, yes, for the sake of Young Mortimer, your lover," King Edward II said.

Everyone except Isabella exited.

"Heavens can witness, I love none but you," Queen Isabella said about her husband. "Thus he breaks away from my embracements. Oh, that my arms could enclose this isle round about, so that I might pull him to me — where I want him. Or that these tears that drizzle from my eyes had the power to mollify his stony heart, so that, when I had him, we might never part!"

The Earl of Lancaster, the Earl of Warwick, Young Mortimer, and others entered the room inside Tynemouth Castle. Much noise from the battle could be heard.

"I wonder how he escaped?" the Earl of Lancaster asked, referring to Gaveston.

"Who's this?" Young Mortimer asked. "The Queen?"

"Yes, Mortimer, the miserable Queen, whose grieving heart her inward sighs have blasted, and whose body with continual mourning is wasted," Queen Isabella said. "These hands of mine are tired with trying to drag my lord away from Gaveston, from wicked Gaveston — and all in vain; for when I speak fair words to my husband, he turns away, and smiles upon his minion."

"Cease to lament, and tell us where's the King," Young Mortimer said.

"What do you want to do with the King?" Queen Isabella asked. "Is it him whom you seek?"

"No, madam, but we seek that cursed Gaveston," the Earl of Lancaster said. "Far be it from the thought of Lancaster to offer violence to his sovereign! We want only to rid the realm of Gaveston. Tell us where he remains, and he shall die."

"He's gone by water to Scarborough," Queen Isabella said. "Pursue him quickly, and he cannot escape. The King has left him, and Gaveston's train of attendants is small."

"Don't delay, sweet Lancaster," the Earl of Warwick said. "Let's march."

"How comes it that the King and Gaveston have parted?" Young Mortimer asked.

"So that this your army, going separate ways, might be of lesser force, and with the army that my husband intends immediately to raise, your army might be easily suppressed," Queen Isabella said. "Therefore, be gone in pursuit of Gaveston."

"Here in the river rides a Flemish hoy, a small fishing ship," Young Mortimer said. "Let's all get aboard, and follow him quickly."

"The wind that bears him away from here will fill our sails," the Earl of Lancaster said. "Come, come on board the ship! It is only an hour's sailing."

"No, Mortimer," Queen Isabella said. "I'll go to my lord the King."

"Nay, rather sail with us to Scarborough," Young Mortimer said.

"You know that the King is so suspicious that, if he just hears I have talked with you, my honor will be called in question," Queen Isabella said. "Therefore, gentle Mortimer, go."

"Madam, I cannot stay to answer you," Young Mortimer said, "but think of Mortimer as he deserves."

Everyone except Queen Isabella exited.

She said to herself, "So well have thou deserved, sweet Mortimer, that Isabel could live with thee forever. In vain I look for love at the hand of Edward, whose eyes are fixed on none but Gaveston. Yet once more I'll beg him with prayers. If he is distant to me and pays no attention to my words, my son and I will go over into France, and to the King my brother — Charles IV of France — there complain about how Gaveston has robbed me of my husband's love. But yet, I hope my sorrows will have an end, and Gaveston shall this blessed day be slain."

— 2.5 —

[Scene 9]

Gaveston, pursued by his enemies, said to himself, "Still, insolent lords, I have escaped your hands, your threats, your alarums, and your hot pursuits. And, although separated from King Edward's eyes, yet Piers of Gaveston lives unambushed and uncaptured by you, breathing in hope — *malgrado* all your beards that muster rebels thus against your King — to see his royal sovereign once again."

"*Malgrado*" is Italian for "despite." The word has a connotation of defiance.

The Earl of Warwick, the Earl of Lancaster, the Earl of Pembroke, and Young Mortimer entered the scene, along with some soldiers. Some attendants also arrived, including James, who served the Earl of Pembroke.

"Set upon him, soldiers," the Earl of Warwick ordered. "Take away his weapons!"

"Thou proud disturber of thy country's peace, corrupter of thy King, cause of these turmoils, base flatterer, yield — give up! — and, were it not for shame, shame and dishonor to a soldier's name, upon my weapon's point here thou should fall, and wallow in thy gore," Young Mortimer said to Gaveston.

In this culture, a high-ranking man would often refrain from killing a low-ranking man, regarding such a deed as beneath him. Young Mortimer, of course, did not regard Gaveston's title of Earl of Cornwall as legitimate.

"Monster of men," the Earl of Lancaster said, "that, like the Greek whore Helen, who despite being legally married to King Menelaus of Sparta ran off with Prince Paris of Troy and lured to arms and bloody wars so many valiant knights, look for no other fortune, wretch, than death! King Edward is not here to buckler — shield and protect — thee."

The Earl of Warwick said, "Lancaster, why are thou talking to the slave?

"Go, soldiers, take the slave away from here; for, by my sword, his head shall come off.

"Gaveston, a short warning of your death shall serve thy needs."

In this Christian culture, condemned prisoners were given some time before their executions to prepare themselves for death.

He continued, "It is our country's cause that here severely we will execute upon thy person. Hang him at a bough."

"My lord!" Gaveston said.

The Earl of Warwick said, "Soldiers, take him away."

Then he said to Gaveston, "Because thou were the favorite of a King, thou shall have this much 'honor' at our hands."

He made a motion for hanging.

"I thank you all, my lords," Gaveston said. "I perceive that beheading is one way for me to die, and hanging is the other, and death is all the same for both of them."

People of the upper classes were beheaded, while people of the lower classes were hung. Traitors were hung, drawn, and quartered. The hanging was in part an insult and in part a way to prolong the traitor's pain since they were hung with a short rope that would not break their neck and give them a quick death.

The Earl of Arundel arrived on the scene as a messenger from King Edward II.

"How are you now, my lord of Arundel?" the Earl of Lancaster asked.

"My lords, King Edward II greets you all by me," the Earl of Arundel said.

"Arundel, say your message," the Earl of Warwick said.

"His majesty, hearing that you have taken Gaveston, begs you, by me, only that he may see Gaveston before he dies because, he says, and he sends you word confirming it, he knows that Gaveston shall die. And, if you gratify his grace as far as allowing him to speak to Gaveston, King Edward II will remember the courtesy."

"What!" the Earl of Warwick said.

Gaveston said, "Renowned Edward, how thy name revives poor Gaveston!"

The Earl of Warwick said, "No, it ought not to revive you. There is no hope that you will live."

"Arundel, we will gratify the King in other matters; he must pardon us in this matter. The answer is no.

"Soldiers, take Gaveston away!"

"Why, my lord of Warwick," Gaveston said. "Won't these delays give birth to my hopes?"

He may have meant that seeing the King would raise his hopes of staying alive, and that then the nobles could have the pleasure of crushing those hopes.

Gaveston continued, "I know it, lords. I know that it is this life you aim to take, yet grant King Edward II his request to see me."

Young Mortimer said to Gaveston, "Shall thou decide what we shall grant?"

He ordered, "Soldiers, take him away!"

He then said to the Earl of Arundel, "To this extent, we'll gratify the King: We'll send Gaveston's head to him by thee. Let him bestow his tears on that, for that is all he gets of Gaveston, or else we'll send him Gaveston's dead, unfeeling trunk."

"No, my lord, lest Edward II bestow more cost in burying Gaveston than Gaveston has ever earned," the Earl of Lancaster said.

"My lords, it is his majesty's request, and by the honor of a King he swears that he will only talk with him and then send him back," the Earl of Arundel said.

"When! Can you tell?" the Earl of Warwick said sarcastically.

In this society, this was a way of scornfully rejecting a proposal, as in our society saying "Yeah! Right!" is.

He continued, "Arundel, no. We know that that man — Edward II — who slackens in the care of the realm, and drives his nobles to these extreme measures for Gaveston, will, if he sees him once, violate any promise in order to possess him."

"Then, if you will not trust his grace with the temporary custody of Gaveston, my lords, I will be the security for his return," the Earl of Arundel said.

The Earl of Arundel was willing to offer his honor as security to the nobles. If he failed to return Gaveston, the Earl of Arundel would lose his honor. This society took honor seriously.

"It is honorable in thee to offer this," Young Mortimer said. "But, because we know thou are a noble gentleman, we will not wrong thee in this way: to make away a true man for a thief."

Young Mortimer did not believe that King Edward II would return Gaveston even if the Earl of Arundel had pledged his honor that Gaveston would be returned. Therefore, Young Mortimer was saying that he would not wrong the Earl of Arundel by allowing him to lose his honor for a thief such as Gaveston.

"What do thou mean, Mortimer?" Gaveston said. "That is overly base, too low, beyond the pale!"

He was objecting to being called a thief.

"Away, base servant, robber of the King's reputation!" Young Mortimer said. "Debate the issue with thy companions and mates."

"My lord Mortimer, and you, my lords, each one, to gratify the King's request therein, concerning the sending of this Gaveston, because his majesty so earnestly desires to see the man before his death, I will upon my honor undertake to carry him and bring him back again," the Earl of Pembroke said, "provided that you, my lord of Arundel, will join with me."

"Pembroke, what will thou do?" the Earl of Warwick asked. "Cause yet more bloodshed? Isn't it enough that we have captured Gaveston, but must we now leave him on 'had I only known,' and let him go?"

"Had I only known" expressed regret for a reckless deed. Taking Gaveston to King Edward II seemed a lot like admitting that the nobles had done wrong in capturing Gaveston.

"My lords, I will not overwoo and beg your honors," the Earl of Pembroke said. "But if you dare trust me, Pembroke, with the prisoner, I give you my oath that I will return him back to you."

"My lord of Lancaster, what do you say about this?" the Earl of Arundel asked.

"Why, I say, let him go on Pembroke's word," the Earl of Lancaster replied.

"And you, lord Mortimer?" the Earl of Pembroke asked.

"What do you say, my lord of Warwick?" Young Mortimer asked.

"Nay, do your pleasures," the Earl of Warwick said. "Do what you want. I know how this will turn out."

"Then give him to me," the Earl of Pembroke said.

"Sweet sovereign, yet I come to see thee before I die!" Gaveston said.

The Earl of Warwick said to himself, "Yet not perhaps, if Warwick's cunning and strategic plan prevail."

"My lord of Pembroke, we deliver him to you," Young Mortimer said. "Return him on your honor. Sound the trumpet! Let's go!"

The trumpet sounded, and everyone exited except the Earl of Pembroke, the Earl of Arundel, Gaveston, and Pembroke's men — James and three other soldiers, who began travelling to King Edward II.

"My lord, you shall go with me," the Earl of Pembroke said to the Earl of Arundel. "My house is not far from here, out of the way a little, but our men shall go along. We who have pretty wenches as our wives, sir, must not come so near and disappoint their lips."

In this society, the word "wench" had a positive, not a negative, connotation.

"It is very kindly spoken, my lord of Pembroke," the Earl of Arundel said. "Your honor has an adamant of power to attract a prince."

An adamant is a magnetic stone; the Earl of Pembroke's hospitality is an adamant of power: It is powerfully attractive.

The Earl of Pembroke said, "Just so, my lord.

"Come here, James. I commit this Gaveston to thee. Be thou this night his keeper; in the morning we will discharge thee of thy charge — we will relieve you of your responsibility. Leave now."

"Unlucky Gaveston, whither are thou going now?" Gaveston asked himself.

As everyone exited, the boy who helped take care of the horses said to Gaveston, "My lord, we'll quickly be at the village of Cobham."

CHAPTER 3

— 3.1 —

[Scene 10]

The Earl of Warwick had been following the Earl of Pembroke, hoping to find an opportunity to take Gaveston from him. Because the Earl of Pembroke was entertaining the Earl of Arundel at his home and so was separated from Gaveston and his guards, the Earl of Warwick and his men now had that opportunity and were surrounding Gaveston, James, and the rest of the Earl of Pembroke's men.

Mourning, Gaveston said, "Oh, treacherous Warwick, thus to wrong thy friend!"

The Earl of Pembroke had pledged his honor to return Gaveston safely to Young Mortimer and the other rebelling lords, but Gaveston could guess that the Earl of Warwick was uninterested in keeping him safe.

"I see it is your life these soldiers pursue," James said.

"Must I fall weaponless, and die in shackles?" Gaveston asked. "Must this day be the end of my life?"

He then said, "Center of all my bliss! If you are men, hurry to the King."

"Center of all my bliss!" referred to King Edward II. He would send help if he knew that the Earl of Warwick had captured Gaveston.

The Earl of Warwick and his company of soldiers entered the scene.

"My lord of Pembroke's men, strive no longer to keep Gaveston," the Earl of Warwick said. "I will have that Gaveston."

"Your lordship does dishonor to yourself and wrong to our lord, the Earl of Pembroke, your honorable friend," James said.

"No, James," the Earl of Warwick said. "It is my country's cause I follow."

He ordered, "Go, take the villain. Soldiers, come away. We'll make quick work."

He said to James, "Commend me to your master, my friend, and tell him that I watched it well."

The Earl of Warwick meant that he had watched well for his opportunity to seize Gaveston.

He then said to Gaveston, "Come, let thy ghost talk with King Edward II."

"Treacherous Earl, shall I not see the King?" Gaveston asked.

The Earl of Warwick replied, "The King of Heaven perhaps, no other King."

He then ordered, "Let's go!"

The Earl of Warwick and his men, with Gaveston, exited. The Earl of Pembroke's men remained behind.

"Come, fellows, it was useless for us to fight to keep Gaveston," James said. "We will go in haste to inform our lord the Earl of Pembroke about what has happened."

— 3.2 —

[Scene 11]

King Edward II, Young Spenser, Baldock, and some soldiers with drums and fifes gathered together.

"I long to hear an answer from the Barons regarding my friend, my dearest Gaveston," King Edward II said. "Ah, Young Spenser, the riches of my realm cannot ransom him. Gaveston is marked to die. I know the malice of the younger Mortimer. I know Warwick is rough, and Lancaster is inexorable, and I shall never see my lovely Piers Gaveston again. The Barons oppose me with their pride."

"If I were King Edward II, England's sovereign, son to the lovely Eleanor of Spain, great Edward Longshanks' son, would I bear these shows of defiance, this rage, and suffer uncontrolled these Barons thus to beard — openly oppose me — in my land, in my own realm?" Young Spenser asked.

To pull a man's beard was a serious insult.

King Edward II's father, Edward I, was called Edward Longshanks because of his height; he was over six feet tall. Edward II's mother was Eleanor of Castile. King Edward II's parents married in 1254.

Young Spenser continued, "My lord, pardon my speech. If you had retained your father's courage and greatness, if you had retained the honor of your name, you would not tolerate like this your majesty being rebuffed by your nobility. Strike off their heads, and let them preach on poles. No doubt, the heads on poles will teach the rest important lessons since by the severed heads' sermons the rest will profit much and learn obedience to their lawful King."

"Yes, gentle Spenser," King Edward II said, "we have been too mild, too kind to them; but now we have drawn our sword, and if they don't send me my Gaveston, we'll steel it on their helmet and poll their tops."

"To steel it on their helmets" means "to strike their helmets with steel swords."

To "poll their tops" literally means to "cut off the top of a tree." King Edward II was saying metaphorically that he would cut off the heads of the rebelling nobles.

"This proud resolve becomes your majesty, not to be tied to their desire, as though your highness were still a schoolboy and must be awed and frightened and governed like a child," Baldock said.

Hugh Spenser, an old man who was the father of Young Spenser, arrived on the scene. Some of his soldiers accompanied him. Hugh Spenser — Spenser Senior — was holding a truncheon, a staff that is a symbol of authority.

Spenser Senior said, "Long live my sovereign, the noble Edward, in peace triumphant, fortunate in wars!"

"Welcome, old man," King Edward II said. "Have you come to give Edward aid? If so, then tell thy Prince from where and who thou are."

"With a band of bowmen and of pikes, brown bills, and targeteers, four hundred strong, sworn to defend King Edward's royal right, I come in person to your majesty," Spenser Senior said.

The bowmen wielded long bows. A pike is a long thrusting spear; they were sometimes set up in front of bowmen to provide a defensive barrier. Brown bills are bronzed halberds. Targeteers carried small round shields that were called targets.

He continued, "I am Spenser Senior, the father of Young Hugh Spenser there. I am bound to your highness everlastingly for favors done to Young Spenser, and therefore to us all."

"Is he thy father, Young Spenser?" King Edward II asked.

"That is true, if it pleases your grace," Young Spenser said. "He pours, in return for all your goodness shown to me, his life, my lord, before your princely feet."

"Welcome ten thousand times, old man, again!" King Edward II said. "Spenser Senior, this love, this kindness to thy King, proves thy noble mind and disposition."

He then said, "Young Spenser, I here create thee Earl of Wiltshire, and daily I will enrich thee with our favor that like the sunshine shall reflect over thee. In addition, the more to demonstrate our love, because we hear Lord Bruce is selling his land and that the Mortimers are in the process of negotiating for it, thou shall have crowns — coins — from us to outbid the Barons. And, Spenser, don't be frugal, but instead lay out the coins."

Lord William de Bruce was arranging a sale of land that the Mortimers were negotiating for, but King Edward II was giving Young Spenser enough money to outbid the Mortimers and purchase the land.

King Edward II said, "Soldiers, a largess, and thrice welcome all!"

King Edward II was saying that he would give Spenser Senior's soldiers a gift of money.

"My lord, here comes the Queen," Young Spenser said.

Queen Isabella, Prince Edward, and Levune, a Frenchman, entered the scene. Prince Edward was the oldest son of King Edward II and Queen Isabella. Levune served as a messenger.

"Madam, what is the news?" King Edward II asked.

"News of dishonor, lord, and of discontent," Queen Isabella replied. "Our friend Levune, faithful and full of trust, informs us, by letters and by oral reports that lord Charles IV — our brother, the King of France — because your highness has been slack in homage, has seized Normandy into his hands.

"These are the letters, and this man is the messenger Levune."

"Welcome, Levune," King Edward II said. "Tush, Sib, if this is all, King Charles IV of France and I will soon be friends again."

"Sib" means "kin." In this context, it means "wife."

He continued, "But about my Gaveston: Shall I never see, never behold thee now?

"Madam, in this matter we will employ you and your little son. You shall go negotiate with the King of France.

"Boy, see you bear yourself bravely to the King, and do your message and mission with a majesty."

"Don't commit to my youth things of more weight than are fitting for a Prince as young as I to bear," Prince Edward said. "And fear not, lord and father. Heaven's great beams on Atlas' shoulder shall not lie more safe than shall your command committed to my trust."

Atlas was a Titan who held up the sky. In Prince Edward's description, Atlas was supporting the sky's roof-beams on his shoulder.

"Ah, boy," Queen Isabella said, "this precociousness makes thy mother fear that thou are not marked to many days on Earth!"

"Madam, we command that you and our son with speed be shipped across the English Channel," King Edward II said. "Levune shall follow you with all the haste that we can dispatch him from here. Choose from our lords some to bear you company, and go in peace; leave us in the wars at home.”

“Unnatural wars, where subjects defy their King,” Queen Isabella said. “May God end them at once and for all! My lord, I take my leave to make my preparations for France.”

Queen Isabella and Prince Edward exited.

The Earl of Arundel entered the scene.

“Lord Arundel, have thou come alone?” King Edward II asked.

“Yes, my good lord, for Gaveston is dead,” the Earl of Arundel said.

“Ah, the traitors. Have they put my friend to death?” King Edward II said. “Tell me, Arundel, did he die before you arrived, or did thou see my friend take his death?”

“Neither, my lord,” the Earl of Arundel replied, “for as Gaveston was ambushed, surrounded all around with weapons and with enemies, I gave your highness’ message to them all, demanding him from them — well, pleading with them — and said, upon the honor of my name, that I would undertake to carry him to your highness, and to bring him back.”

“And tell me, would the rebels deny me that?” King Edward II asked.

“Proud recreants!” Young Spenser said.

“Yes, Spenser, traitors all!” King Edward II said.

“I found them at first unyielding,” the Earl of Arundel said. “The Earl of Warwick would not listen to me, Mortimer hardly; Pembroke and Lancaster spoke least. And when they flatly had denied my request, refusing to accept my pledge for him, the Earl of Pembroke mildly and gently thus spoke: ‘My lords, because our sovereign sends for him and promises that Gaveston shall be safely returned, I will undertake this: to take him away from here to see the King and then to see him redelivered to your hands.’”

“Well, and how does it happen that Gaveston did not come here?” King Edward II asked.

“Some treason or some villainy was the cause,” Young Spenser said.

“The Earl of Warwick seized Gaveston as he was on his way here,” the Earl of Arundel said. “After delivering Gaveston to his men, the Earl of Pembroke rode home, thinking that his prisoner was safe. But before he returned, Warwick lay in ambush, and took Gaveston to his death, and in a trench struck off his head, and marched to the camp.”

"A bloody deed, flatly against the law of arms," Young Spenser said.

"Shall I speak, or shall I sigh and die!" King Edward II said.

"My lord, assign your vengeance to the sword upon these Barons," Young Spenser said. "Hearten up your men. Let the rebelling nobles not unrevenged murder your friends. Raise your standards, Edward, in the battlefield, and march to use fire to smoke them from their starting-holes."

Hunters used smoke to force animals from their starting holes, aka places of refuge.

King Edward II knelt and said, "By Earth, the common mother of us all, by Heaven, and by all the moving orbs thereof, by this right hand, and by my father's sword, and by all the honors belonging to my crown, I will have heads and lives for Gaveston — as many as I have manors, castles, towns, and towers!"

In the Ptolemaic conception of the universe, the Earth is at the center of the universe and is surrounded by moving orbs — aka spheres — that contain the Moon, the Sun, each of the planets, and the fixed stars.

King Edward II rose and said, "Treacherous Warwick! Traitorous Mortimer! If I am England's King, in lakes of gore your headless trunks, your bodies will I trail, so that you may drink your fill, and quaff in blood, and I will stain my royal standard with the same, so that my bloody banners may suggest remembrance of revenge immortally on your accursed traitorous progeny, you villains who have slain my Gaveston!

"And in this place of honor and of trust, Spenser, sweet Spenser, I adopt thee here. Young Spenser will take Gaveston's place. And purely of our love we do create thee Earl of Gloucester and Lord Chamberlain, in spite of the times, in spite of enemies."

Seeing a messenger, Young Spenser said, "My lord, here's a messenger from the Barons who desires access to your majesty."

"Admit him near," King Edward II said.

The Barons' herald, with his coat of arms, came near and said, "Long live King Edward II, England's lawful lord!"

"Those who sent thee here certainly do not wish a long life for me," King Edward II said. "Thou come from Young Mortimer and his accomplices. A ranker rout — band — of rebels never was. Well, say thy message."

"The Barons up in arms by me salute your highness with long life and happiness," the herald said, "and they bid me say, as one who delivers an official complaint to your grace, that if without shedding of blood you wish to remedy the complaint of the rebelling lords, you will remove from your princely person this Young Spenser — this putrifying branch that kills the royal vine, whose golden leaves encircle your princely head, your diadem — your crown."

King Edward II's crown was decorated with strawberry leaves. Strawberry plants are not vines, although they may appear to be because they produce runners, aka daughter plants.

The herald continued, "The Barons up in arms say that such pernicious, dangerous upstarts dim the brightness of your crown, and they lovingly advise your grace to cherish virtue and nobility and to have old advisors who are held in high esteem, and shake off obsequious, false-faced, deceiving flatterers.

"This granted, they, their honors, and their lives are to your highness vowed and dedicated."

"Ah, traitors, will they still display their pride!" Young Spenser said.

King Edward II said to the herald, "Leave! Don't wait for an answer, but be gone! Rebels! Will they decide for their sovereign his entertainment, his pleasures, and his company? Yet, before thou go, see how I divorce Spenser from me."

King Edward II embraced Young Spenser.

He continued, "Now get thee to thy lords, and tell them I will come to chastise them for murdering Gaveston. Hurry thee! Get thee gone! Edward with fire and sword follows at thy heels."

The herald exited.

King Edward II said to Young Spenser, "My lord, do you see how these rebels swell with pride?"

He added, "Soldiers, good hearts, defend your sovereign's right, for now, even now, we march to make them stoop and bow down before us.

"Let's go!"

— 3.3 —

[Scene 12]

The battle was taking place with alarums, excursions, a great fight, and a retreat.

King Edward II, Spenser Senior, Young Spenser, and the noblemen on the King's side gathered together.

"Why do we sound retreat?" King Edward II said. "Attack them, lords! This day I shall pour vengeance with my sword on those proud rebels who are up in arms and confront and oppose their King."

"I don't doubt it, my lord," Young Spenser said. "Right will prevail."

"It is not amiss, my liege, for both sides to rest a while and catch their breath," Spenser Senior said. "Our men, with sweat and dust all well-near choked, begin to faint because of heat, and this withdrawal refreshes horse and man."

"Here come the rebels," Young Spenser said.

Young Mortimer, the Earl of Lancaster, the Earl of Warwick, the Earl of Pembroke, and other rebels entered the scene.

This was not a parley; instead, the two groups had come close to each other by chance.

"Look, Lancaster, yonder is Edward II among his flatterers," Young Mortimer said.

"And there let him be," the Earl of Lancaster said, "until he pays dearly for their company."

"And he shall pay dearly, or Warwick's sword shall smite in vain," the Earl of Warwick said.

"What, rebels, do you shrink and sound retreat?" King Edward II shouted.

"No, Edward, no," Young Mortimer said. "Thy flatterers faint and flee."

The Earl of Lancaster said to King Edward II, "Thou should best at once forsake them and their intrigues, for they'll betray thee, traitors as they are."

"I throw the word 'traitor' back in thy face, rebellious Lancaster," Young Spenser said.

"Go away, base upstart!" the Earl of Pembroke said. "Do thou insult nobles thus?"

"Is it not a noble attempt and honorable deed, do you think, to assemble aid and levy arms against your lawful King?" Spenser Senior asked.

"For which, before long, their heads shall atone to appease the wrath of their offended King," King Edward II said.

"So then, Edward, thou will fight to the last and would rather bathe thy sword in your subjects' blood than banish that pernicious company," Young Mortimer said.

"Yes, traitors all," King Edward II said. "Rather than thus be insulted, I will make England's municipal towns huge heaps of stones and make plows go about our palace gates."

Because these centers of civilization would be destroyed by war, their sites would become farmland.

"A desperate and unnatural resolution," the Earl of Warwick said. "Sound the alarum to the fight! Saint George for England, and the Barons' right!"

"Saint George for England, and King Edward's right!" King Edward II said.

Saint George is the patron saint of England.

The two parties exited in different directions.

— 3.4 —

[Scene 13]

The battle was over, and King Edward II's army was victorious. His captives included the Earl of Warwick, the Earl of Lancaster, and Young Mortimer. King Edward II, Young Spenser, Spenser Senior, and some soldiers on the King's side were present. The Earl of Kent was also present.

"Now, insolent lords," King Edward II said, "now not by chance and luck of war, but by justice of the quarrel and the cause, lowered and humbled is your pride. I think you hang your heads, but we'll promote them, traitors."

He meant that he would promote — raise — their heads by cutting them off, sticking them on poles, and displaying them in a high place where people could see them.

He added, "Now it is time to be avenged on you for all your insults, and for the murder of my dearest friend, to whom right well you knew our soul was knit — good Piers of Gaveston, my sweet favorite. Rebels, recreants, traitors, you killed him!"

The Earl of Kent said, "Brother, for the good of thee and of thy land, they removed that flatterer from thy throne."

"So, sir, you have spoken," King Edward II said. "Go away, leave our presence!"

The Earl of Kent exited.

King Edward II continued, "Accursed wretches, was it for the good of us, when we had sent our messenger to request that Gaveston might be spared to come to speak with us, and Pembroke undertook to be responsible for his return, that thou, proud Warwick, kept watch over the prisoner, poor Piers, and beheaded him against the law of arms? For which thy head shall overlook the rest as much as thou in rage outdid the rest."

King Edward II was saying that the Earl of Warwick's head would be set in a higher place on the London Bridge than the heads of the other rebels.

"Tyrant, I scorn thy threats and menaces," the Earl of Warwick said. "It is only temporal, worldly punishment that thou can inflict."

"The worst you can inflict on us is death," the Earl of Lancaster said, "and it is better to die and live in Heaven than live in infamy under such a King as you are."

"Away with them, Spenser Senior, my lord of Winchester!" King Edward II said.

He continued, "I command you without hesitation to cut off the heads of these lusty leaders, Warwick and Lancaster! Take them away!"

"Farewell, vain world!" the Earl of Warwick said.

"Sweet Mortimer, farewell!" the Earl of Lancaster said.

The Earl of Warwick and the Earl of Lancaster exited in the custody of Spenser Senior.

"England, unkind to thy nobility, groan for this grief," Young Mortimer said. "Behold how thou are maimed!"

"Go, take that haughty Young Mortimer to the Tower of London," King Edward II ordered. "There see him safely bestowed, and as for the others, do speedy execution on them all. Be gone!"

Young Mortimer said, "What, Mortimer? Can rough stony walls confine thy manly virtue that aspires to heaven?

"No, Edward, England's scourge, it may not be. Mortimer's hope far surmounts his fortune."

Young Mortimer exited in the custody of guards.

"Sound drums and trumpets. March with me, my friends," King Edward II said. "Edward this day has crowned himself King anew."

King Edward II exited, leaving behind Young Spenser, Levune, and Baldock.

Young Spenser said, "Levune, the trust that we place in thee will produce quiet in King Edward's land. Therefore, be gone in haste, and with care bestow that treasure on the lords of France, so that, therewith all enchanted, like the guard who allowed Jove to pass in showers of gold to Danaë, all aid may be denied to Queen Isabel, who now in France makes friends, intending to cross the seas and come back to England with her young son, and step into his father's rule."

According to rumor, Queen Isabella was plotting to overthrow her husband: King Edward II. Therefore, Young Spenser wanted Levune to bribe some French noblemen in the King of France's court to stop Queen Isabella from getting French help.

"That's what these Barons and the cunning Queen have been aiming at," Levune said.

"Yes, but, Levune, thou see these Barons lay their heads on blocks together," Baldock said. "What they intend, the hangman — the executioner — frustrates completely."

"Don't have any doubts, my lords," Levune said. "I'll shake hands with and strike such bargains so secretly among the lords of France with England's gold that Isabel shall make her complaints in vain, and the King of France shall be obdurate with her tears."

"Then make for France at once," Young Spenser said. "Levune, away! Proclaim King Edward II's wars and victories."

CHAPTER 4
— 4.1 —
[Scene 14]

Near the Tower of London, the Earl of Kent, the King's half-brother, who had been exiled from the royal court, said to himself, "Fair blows the wind for France. Blow, gentle gale, until Edmund has arrived in France for England's good! Nature, yield to my country's cause in this! A brother, no, but a butcher of thy friends, proud Edward, do thou banish me from thy presence? But I'll go to France and cheer the wronged Queen and inform her of Edward's looseness."

"Edmund" is the Earl of Kent's name.

The word "looseness" referred to immoral conduct both in politics and in sexual relations.

The Earl of Kent continued, "Unnatural King, to slaughter noblemen and cherish flatterers. Young Mortimer, I await thy sweet escape. Gracious, gloomy night, be helpful to his plot."

Young Mortimer, disguised, entered the scene and asked, "Holla, who walks there? Is it you, my lord?"

"Yes, Mortimer, it is I," the Earl of Kent replied. "But has thy potion worked so happily?"

Young Mortimer had drugged his keepers' wine with sedatives.

"It has, my lord," Young Mortimer answered. "The warders — all asleep, I thank them — allowed me to pass in peace. But has your grace got us a ship to take us to France?"

"Don't fear that I haven't," the Earl of Kent replied.

— 4.2 —

[Scene 15]

Queen Isabella and Prince Edward talked together.

"Ah, boy, all our friends fail us in France," Queen Isabella said. "The lords are cruel, and the King is unkind to his kindred. What shall we do?"

"Madam, return to England and please my father well," Prince Edward said, "and then give a fig for all my uncle's friendship here in France."

His uncle, King Charles IV of France, was declining to help Isabella. "To give someone the fig" was to make a certain obscene gesture at that person.

He continued, "I guarantee you that I'll win his highness King Edward II quickly. He loves me better than a thousand Spensers."

"Ah, boy, thou are deceived, at least in this: to think that we can still be tuned together and made harmonious," Queen Isabella said. "No, no, we jar too much to be reconciled.

"Unkind King Charles IV of France! Unhappy Isabel, when France rejects me, where, oh, where will thou direct thy steps? What should I do next?"

Sir John of Hainault entered the room and asked, "Madam, how are you?"

"Ah, good Sir John of Hainault," Queen Isabella said. "I have never been so cheerless nor been so far distressed!"

"I hear, sweet lady, of the King's unkindness," Sir John of Hainault said, "but don't droop, madam. Noble minds scorn despair. Will your grace go with me to the county of Hainault in the Low Countries, and there await an advantageous time with your son?"

He then said to Prince Edward, "What do you say, my lord? Will you go with your friends, and all of us equally cast off all our hope that we had of getting aid from the King of France?"

"As long as it pleases the Queen my mother, it pleases me," Prince Edward replied. "Neither the King of England, nor the court of France, shall move me from my gracious mother's side until I am strong enough to break a quarterstaff in battle, and then I will strike at the proudest Spenser's head."

"Well said, my lord," Sir John of Hainault said.

"Oh, my sweetheart, how do I mourn the wrongs done to thee, yet triumph in the hope of thee, my joy!" Queen Isabella said to her son.

She then said, "Ah, sweet Sir John, even to the furthest limit of Europe, on the shore of Tanais, we would go with thee, and so we will go with thee to Hainault, so we will."

Tanais is the Latin name of Russia's Don River, which the Elizabethans regarded as being the boundary between Europe and Asia.

Queen Isabella continued, "The Marquis of Hainault, your brother, is a noble gentleman. His grace, I dare presume, will welcome me.

"But who are these men coming toward us?"

The Earl of Kent and Young Mortimer walked toward them.

"Madam, long may you live," the Earl of Kent said, "much happier than your friends in England do."

"Lord Edmund and lord Mortimer! Still alive!" Queen Isabella said. "Welcome to France."

She said to Young Mortimer, "The news came here, my lord, that you were dead, or very near your death."

"Lady, the last was truest of the two," Young Mortimer said, "but Mortimer, reserved for better fortune, has shaken off the captivity of the Tower of London."

He turned to Prince Edward and said, "And he lives to advance your standard, my good lord."

"What do you mean?" Prince Edward said. "The King my father still lives! No, my lord Mortimer, not I, I assure you."

Prince Edward heard "advance your standard," which means "raise your banner in battle," and immediately realized that Young Mortimer was talking of invading England and fighting against King Edward II, Prince Edward's father. He did not want that. He did not want to become King of England while his father was still alive.

"Not, son! Why not?" Queen Isabella said. "I wish it would be no worse than putting you on the throne. But, gentle lords, we are friendless in France."

"Monsieur le Grand, a noble friend of yours, told us, at our arrival, all the news," Young Mortimer said. "How hard the nobles, how unkind the King of France has shown himself to you, but madam, right makes room where weapons are lacking."

His words were ambiguous. They could mean 1) right finds a way to succeed in a situation where weapons for its side are lacking, or 2) right must retreat in a situation where weapons for its side are lacking.

He continued, "And, although many friends have been killed, such as the Earl of Warwick and the Earl of Lancaster, as have others of our party and faction, yet we have friends, I assure your grace, in England who would toss up their caps and clap their hands for joy to see us there equipped to battle our foes."

"I wish that all were well, and Edward well reformed, for England's honor, peace, and quietness," the Earl of Kent said.

"But by the sword, my lord, it must be earned," Young Mortimer said. "King Edward II will never forsake his flatterers."

Sir John of Hainault said, "My lords of England, since the unchivalrous King of France refuses to give aid of arms to this distressed Queen, his sister, here, go with her to Hainault. Don't doubt that we will find comfort, money, men, and friends before long to bid the English King a base."

He was referring to a game called prisoner's base, but his words "to bid the English King a base" meant "to challenge King Edward II to an encounter in which there is danger." He may have meant that he wanted King Edward II to leave his home base and come out and fight.

The game prisoner's base involved lots of running and the danger of being captured by the other team. "To bid a base" means to challenge a player to make a run. Also, "to bid the English King a base" includes a pun: "to bid the English King abase himself."

Sir John of Hainault asked, "Tell me, young Prince Edward, what do you think of the game?"

"I think King Edward II will outrun us all," Prince Edward replied.

"No, son, that is not so; and you must not discourage your friends who are so eager to come to your aid," Queen Isabella said.

"Sir John of Hainault, pardon us, please," the Earl of Kent said. "These comforts that you give our woeful Queen bind us all in kindness at your command."

"Yes, Kent, gentle brother-in-law, and may the God of Heaven prosper your happy proposal, good Sir John," Queen Isabella said.

"This noble gentleman, eager to fight, was born, I see, to be our anchor-hold," Young Mortimer said. "Sir John of Hainault, be it to thy renown that England's Queen and nobles in distress have been by thee restored and comforted."

"Madam, and you, my lords, come along with me so that England's peers may Hainault's welcome see," Sir John said.

— 4.3 —

[Scene 16]

King Edward II, the Earl of Arundel, Young Spenser, and Spenser Senior met together. Others were present.

King Edward II said, "Thus, after many threats of wrathful war, England's Edward triumphs with his friends, and may Edward continue to triumph with his friends uncontrolled and without censure."

Despite recent success, he still faced challenges from enemies.

"My lord of Gloucester — Young Spenser — do you hear the news?" King Edward II asked.

"What news, my lord?" Young Spenser asked.

"Why, man, they say there is great execution — much killing — done throughout the realm," King Edward II replied.

He then asked, "My lord of Arundel, you have the official list, don't you?"

"From the lieutenant of the Tower of London, my lord," the Earl of Arundel said.

"Please, let us see it," King Edward II said.

He took the list and then gave it to Young Spenser, saying, "Read it, Spenser."

Young Spenser read out loud the names of those who had been executed.

King Edward II said, "Why, so it is. They embarked quickly on a journey to the afterlife a month ago. Now, on my life, they'll neither bark nor bite."

Some time had passed since the battle. After the battle, many traitors had been executed.

King Edward II continued, "Now, sirs, the news from France.

"Gloucester, I am confident that the lords of France love England's gold so well that Isabella gets no aid from thence.

"What now remains to be done? Have you proclaimed, my lord, a reward for those who can bring in Young Mortimer?"

Young Spenser, who was the Earl of Gloucester, replied, "My lord, we have; and, if he is in England, he will be captured before long, I don't doubt."

"*If,* do thou say?" King Edward II said. "Young Spenser, it is as true as death that he is on England's ground; our harbor-masters are not so careless of their King's command."

King Edward II believed that Young Mortimer was still in England because the harbor-masters would keep him from sailing to France.

A messenger arrived.

"How is it now?" King Edward II asked. "What is the news with thee? From where comes this news?"

The messenger said, "I have letters, my lord, and tidings from out of France. To you, my lord of Gloucester, I have a letter from Levune."

"Read it," King Edward II said.

Young Spenser read the letter from Levune out loud:

"*My duty to your honor* — etc. I will skip reading out loud the formal introduction — *I have, according to instructions in that behalf, dealt with the King of France's lords, and brought it about that the Queen, all discontented and discouraged, has gone out of France; to where, if you ask, she has gone with Sir John of Hainault, brother to the Marquis of Hainault, into Flanders. With them have gone lord Edmund and the lord Young Mortimer, having in their company various people of your nation, and others; and, as reliable and consistent report goes, they intend to give King Edward II battle in England sooner than he can look for them. This is all the news of importance. Your honor's in all service, Levune.*"

"Ah, villains, has that Young Mortimer escaped from England?" King Edward II said. "With him has Edmund, my brother, the Earl of Kent, gone as an associate? And will Sir John of Hainault lead the round?"

The round is a dance in which dancers form a circle. Sir John of Hainault's brother, the Marquis of Hainault, would give much aid to Queen Isabella so she could invade England.

King Edward II added, "Welcome, in God's name, madam and your son. England shall welcome you and all your rout of followers. Gallop your Sun-chariot quickly, bright Phoebus Apollo, through the sky, and, dusky Night, do the same in a rusty iron car. Between you both, shorten the time, I pray, so that I may see that most desired day when we may meet these traitors in the field of battle.

"Ah, nothing grieves me except that my little boy — Prince Edward — is thus misled to support their evil deeds.

"Come, friends, to Bristol, there to make us a strong army.

"And, winds, be as even-handed to bring our enemies back to England, as you were injurious to bear them away from England."

— 4.3 —

[Scene 17]

Queen Isabella, Prince Edward, the Earl of Kent, Young Mortimer, and Sir John of Hainault talked together in Harwich, a port-town in southeast England.

"Now lords, our loving friends and countrymen," Queen Isabella said, "welcome to England, all of you, with favorable winds. We have left our kindest friends in Belgia so we can battle friends and relatives in England, our home."

Belgia was then part of the Netherlands; now it is part of Belgium. It is the location of Hainaut.

She continued, "This is a heavy case, a sad predicament, when force to force is knit, and sword and glaive — sword and spear — in civil wars make kin and countrymen slaughter themselves in others, and their sides with their own weapons gored!"

In civil war, people kill their fellow citizens, sometimes including their relatives, thereby killing a part of themselves.

She continued, "But what's the remedy? Misgoverning, lawless, immoral Kings are the cause of all this ruin; and, Edward II, thou are one among them all whose looseness — laxness and lewdness — has betrayed thy land to spoil and made the gutters overflow with blood. Of thine own people you should be the protector and father-figure, but thou ..."

"Nay, madam, if you are to be a warrior, you must not grow so passionate in speeches," Young Mortimer said.

In this culture, people believed that showing extreme passion and being unable to control one's emotions were signs of weakness.

Young Mortimer continued, "Lords, since we have, by the consent of providential Heaven arrived and armed in Prince Edward's right, here for our country's cause let us swear to him all homage, fealty, and zeal.

"And as for the open wrongs and injuries that Edward II has done to us, his Queen, and land, we come in arms to work destruction for them with the sword, so that England's Queen in peace may repossess her dignities and honors — and moreover so that we may remove from the King these flatterers who havoc and waste England's wealth and treasury."

"Let the trumpets sound, my lord, and let us march forward," Sir John of Hainault said. "If we stay here talking, Edward II will think we come to flatter him."

"I wish that he had never been flattered more than we have flattered him," the Earl of Kent said.

He believed that the flattery of such people as Gaveston and the Spensers had greatly harmed King Edward II.

<h1 style="text-align:center">— 4.5 —</h1>

<h1 style="text-align:center">[Scene 18]</h1>

King Edward II, Baldock, and Young Spenser talked together.

"Flee, flee, my lord," Young Spenser said. "The Queen's forces are very strong. Her friends multiply, and yours fail. Let us steer our way to Ireland, there to breathe and rest awhile."

"Was I born to flee and run away, and leave the Mortimers behind me as conquerors?" King Edward II said. "Give me my horse, and let's encourage our troops, and in this bed of honor die with fame."

"Oh, no, my lord, this princely resolution is not suitable for the time," Baldock said. "Let's leave! We are pursued!"

They exited.

Alone, the Earl of Kent immediately entered the scene. He was carrying a sword and a target — a small, round shield.

He said to himself, "King Edward II fled this way, but I have come too late. Edward, alas, my heart relents for thee.

"Proud traitor, Mortimer, why do thou chase thy lawful King, thy sovereign, with thy sword? Vile wretch!

"And why have thou — I, myself — most unnatural of all because I oppose my brother, borne arms against thy brother and thy King? May showers of vengeance rain on my cursed head, I pray to God, to Whom in justice it belongs to punish this unnatural revolt.

"Edward II, this Mortimer aims at thy life. Oh, flee from him, then! But, Edmund, Earl of Kent, you must calm this rage. Dissemble, or thou die."

The Earl of Kent was saying that he needed to pretend that he had kind feelings for the rebellion of Queen Isabella and Young Mortimer.

He continued, "Young Mortimer and Isabel kiss while they conspire, and yet she bears a face of love in truth."

He was being sarcastic. Adultery is not love in truth.

The Earl of Kent, whose name was Edmund, continued, "Shame on that love which hatches death and hate.

"Edmund, run away!

"The town of Bristol to Longshanks' blood — his son Edward II — is false; it has gone over to the Queen's side.

"I must not be found alone, by myself, in case I arouse suspicion. Proud Mortimer pries closely into my movements."

Before he could leave, Queen Isabella, Young Mortimer, Prince Edward, and Sir John of Hainault entered the scene.

Queen Isabella said, "The God of Kings gives successful battles to them who fight with right on their side and who fear God's wrath. Since then successfully we have prevailed, may thanks be given to Heaven's great architect and to you, my allies.

"Before we farther proceed, my noble lords, we here create our well-beloved son Lord Warden of the Realm, out of love and care for his royal person, and since the Fates have made his father so unfortunate."

Because King Edward II was still alive, Prince Edward could not yet be made King.

The Queen added, "Proceed in this — the affairs of England — my lords, my loving lords, as seems fittest to all your wisdoms."

"Madam, if I may ask without offense, how will you deal with Edward in his fall?" the Earl of Kent asked Queen Isabella.

"Tell me, good uncle, which Edward do you mean?" Prince Edward asked the Earl of Kent.

He was saying that the Earl of Kent ought to use Edward II's title of King.

"Nephew," the Earl of Kent answered, "I mean your father; I dare not call him King."

"My lord of Kent, what is the need for these questions?" Young Mortimer asked. "It is not in the Queen's power and control nor in ours to dispose of Edward II; instead, your brother shall be disposed of as the realm and Parliament shall please."

He said quietly to Queen Isabella, "I don't like this relenting, pitying mood in Edmund, Earl of Kent. Madam, it is good to keep a close eye on him earlier rather than later."

He was worried that the Earl of Kent might change loyalties.

Queen Isabella said to the Earl of Kent, "My lord, the Mayor of Bristol knows our mind. He knows our intentions."

"Yes, madam," Young Mortimer said, "and they who fled the battlefield will not easily escape. The Mayor of Bristol's men will round them up."

"Baldock is with the King," Queen Isabella said. "He's an excellent Chancellor, isn't he, my lord?"

She was sarcastic, as could be told by her tone.

"So are the Spensers: the father and the son," Sir John of Hainault replied.

He was sarcastic, as could be told by his tone.

The Earl of Kent said, "This Edward II is the ruin of the realm."

He was sarcastic, although no one could tell by his tone.

Rice ap Howell and the Mayor of Bristol arrived with Spenser Senior as their prisoner. A Welshman, Rice ap Howell had been a prisoner in the Tower of London until Queen Isabella freed him.

Rice ap Howell said, "May God save Queen Isabel and her princely son!

"Madam, the Mayor and citizens of Bristol, in sign of love and duty to this royal presence of Prince Edward, present by me this traitor to the state: Spenser Senior, the father to that wanton Young Spenser, who, like the lawless Catiline of Rome, reveled in England's wealth and treasury."

Catiline was accused of conspiring to overthrow the Roman Republic. In 62 B.C.E., he died in battle. Both Spensers were accused of enriching themselves with the royal treasury.

"We thank you all," Queen Isabella said.

"Your loving care in this deserves princely favors and rewards," Young Mortimer said. "But where have the King and the other Spenser fled?"

"Spenser the son, who was created Earl of Gloucester, is with that smooth-tongued, flattering scholar Baldock," Rice ap Howell said. "Recently, they boarded ship with King Edward II for Ireland."

"May some whirlwind fetch them back, or sink them all," Young Mortimer said. "They shall be driven from cover there, I don't doubt."

"Shall I not yet see the King my father?" Prince Edward asked.

"Unhappy Edward, chased from England's territory," the Earl of Kent said quietly to himself.

"Madam, what remains to be done?" Sir John of Hainault asked. "Why are you in such a thoughtful muse?"

"I grieve over my lord and husband's ill fortune," Queen Isabella said. "But, sadly, care of — concern for — my country called me to this war!"

"Madam, have done with worry and sad complaint," Young Mortimer said. "Your King has wronged your country and himself, and we must seek to right it as we may."

He ordered, "Meanwhile, take this rebel to the block to be beheaded."

He then said to Spenser Senior, "Your lordship cannot privilege your head."

As the Earl of Wiltshire, Spenser Senior was a nobleman and so would not be hung as a commoner would; instead, he would be beheaded. Having high status would not keep him from being killed.

Spenser Senior said, "A rebel is he who fights against his Prince: King Edward II. Those who fought for Edward II's rights did not rebel against him."

"Take him away," Young Mortimer said. "He prattles."

Guards took away Spenser Senior.

Young Mortimer said, "You, Rice ap Howell, shall do good service to her majesty. Being of high standing in your country — Wales — here, you will follow these rebellious renegades."

He then said to Queen Isabella, "We in the meanwhile, madam, must carefully deliberate about how Baldock, Young Spenser, and their accomplices may in their fall from power be pursued to their deaths."

— 4.6 —

[Scene 19]

On 16 November 1326, the Abbot of Neath, King Edward II, Young Spenser, and Baldock talked together. Some monks were present. The royal party was in hiding at Neath Abbey in south Wales. King Edward II, Young Spenser, and Baldock were disguised as monks.

"Have no doubt, my lord," the Abbot of Neath said. "Have no fear. As silent and as careful will we be to keep your royal person safe with us, free from suspicion and free from deadly invasion from such people as are pursuing your majesty, yourself, and those of your chosen company, as the danger of this stormy time requires."

"Father, thy face should harbor no deceit," King Edward II said. "Oh, if thou had ever been a King, thy heart, pierced deeply with sense of my distress, could not but have compassion for my state.

"Stately and proud in riches and in attendants, once I was powerful and full of pomp, but who is he whom rule and empire have not in life or death made miserable?

"Come, Young Spenser, Baldock, come, sit down by me. Now test that philosophy that in our famous nurseries of arts — Oxford and Cambridge — thou sucked from Plato and from Aristotle."

Plato and Aristotle were ancient Greek philosophers. The contemplative life was much praised in medieval philosophy and in religious works such as Saint Augustine's *City of God*. Kings led an active life, while monks led a contemplative life filled with religious devotion.

King Edward II continued, "Father, this contemplative life is Heaven. Oh, that I might lead this life in quiet, but we, alas, are chased. And my friends, they pursue your lives and my dishonor. Yet, gentle monks, not for treasure, nor for gold, nor for fee, do you betray us and our company."

"Your grace may sit safe and secure, if none but we know of your abode," a monk said.

"No one alive," Young Spenser said, "but fearfully I suspect a gloomy fellow in a meadow outside the abbey. He gave a long look after us, my lord, and all the land, I know, is up in arms, arms that pursue our lives with deadly hate."

"We were embarked for Ireland," Baldock said. "With unfavorable winds and severe tempests, we were driven to fall on shore and become grounded, and here to pine in fear of Mortimer and his confederates."

"Mortimer! Who talks about Mortimer?" King Edward II said. "Who wounds me with the name of Mortimer, that bloodthirsty man? Good father, on thy lap I lay this head of mine, filled with much worry and care. Oh, that I might never open these eyes again, never again lift up this drooping head — oh, nevermore lift up this dying heart!"

"Look up, my lord," Young Spenser said. "Baldock, this drowsiness bodes no good: It is an evil omen."

Seeing men coming, he said, "Even here in this abbey we are betrayed."

Rice ap Howell, the Earl of Leicester, and a mower entered the scene. They were armed with Welsh hooks, a hedging tool that consisted of a long handle with a curved blade on one end: It resembled a scythe. A mower was a man who cut grass and hay with a scythe. The mower was the "gloomy fellow" whom Baldock had seen earlier. Holding a scythe, he looked like the personification of Death.

"Upon my life, those are the men you seek," the mower said.

"Fellow, enough," Rice ap Howell said to the mower.

He said to the Earl of Leicester, "My lord, please be short. Let's get this arrest over quickly."

He then said to all present, "A valid commission authorizes what we do."

The Earl of Leicester said to himself, "He has the Queen's commission, which Young Mortimer persuaded her to make. What cannot gallant Mortimer do with the Queen?"

The word "gallant" means both "bold" and "lover."

He continued, "It's a pity: See where King Edward II sits and hopes to escape unseen the hands of those who seek by force to take away his life. Too true it is: *Quem dies vidit veniens superbum, hunc dies vidit fugiens jacentem.*"

The Latin quotation, which is from Seneca's play *Thyestes*, means, "Him whom the rising Sun has seen exalted in his pride, the setting Sun has seen downfallen."

The Earl of Leicester continued to say to himself, "But, Leicester, cease to grow so passionate and compassionate. Control your feelings."

He then said out loud, "Young Spenser and Baldock, by no other names, I arrest you of high treason here."

He was declining to address them by the titles that King Edward II had given them. Young Spenser was Earl of Gloucester and Lord Chamberlain, and Baldock was the King's Chancellor.

The Earl of Leicester continued, "Don't insist on my using your titles, but obey thy arrest. It is in the name of Isabel the Queen."

He then asked King Edward II, "My lord, why droop you thus?"

"Oh, day, the last of all my bliss on Earth, center of all misfortune!" King Edward II said. "Oh, my stars, why do you frown unkindly on a King? Does the Earl of Leicester come then in Isabella's name to take my life, my company, from me? Here, man, rip up this panting breast and palpitating heart of mine. Take my heart, and let it be the ransom for letting my friends go."

"Away with them!" Rice ap Howell said.

"It may do thee honor yet to let us take our farewell of his grace the King," Young Spenser said.

"My heart with pity grieves to see this sight: a King forced to bear these words and arrogant commands," the Abbot of Neath said.

"Spenser, ah, sweet Young Spenser, thus then we must part," King Edward II said.

"We must, my lord," Young Spenser said. "So the angry heavens command it to be."

"No, so command Hell and cruel Mortimer," King Edward II said. "The gentle heavens have nothing to do with this."

"My lord, it is in vain to grieve or storm in protest," Baldock said. "Here humbly of your grace we take our leaves. Our lots are cast, and I fear, so is thine."

"In Heaven we may meet again, but on Earth we shall never meet," King Edward II said.

He then asked, "Earl of Leicester, tell us, what shall become of us?"

"Your majesty must go to Killingworth Castle in Warwickshire," the Earl of Leicester replied.

"Must!" King Edward II said. "It is somewhat hard when Kings *must* go."

"Here is a litter ready for your grace, awaiting your pleasure, and the day grows old," the Earl of Leicester said.

A litter is a portable bed carried by people.

"It is as good to be gone as to stay and be overtaken by night," Rice ap Howell said.

"A litter have thou?" King Edward II said. "A bed for me to be carried in? Lay me in a coffin, and convey me away from here to the gates of Hell. Let Pluto's bells ring out my fatal death knell, and let hags howl for my death at Charon's shore."

Pluto is the god of the Land of the Dead, and Charon is the ferryman who ferries souls to the Land of the Dead.

King Edward II continued, "For friends has Edward none but these" — he pointed to the monks — "and these" — he pointed to Young Spenser and Baldock — "and these two must die under a tyrant's sword."

"My lord, let's be going," Rice ap Howell said. "Don't care for these, for we shall see them shorter by the heads."

In other words, Young Spenser and Baldock will be beheaded.

"Well, what shall be, shall be," King Edward II said. "Part we must. Sweet Spenser, gentle Baldock, part we must."

Taking off his disguise, he said, "Away, feigned clothing! Unfeigned are my woes."

He said to the Abbot of Neath, "Father, farewell."

He then said, "Earl of Leicester, thou are waiting for me, and go I must. Life, I say farewell to you, along with my friends."

King Edward II and the Earl of Leicester exited.

"Oh, has he gone?" Young Spenser said. "Has noble Edward gone, departed from here, never to see us anymore?

"Heavens, tear yourself to pieces, and fireball that is the Sun, forsake thy orbit! Earth, melt to air! Gone is my sovereign. Gone, gone, alas, never to make return."

"Young Spenser, I see our souls departing from here," Baldock said. "We are deprived of the sunshine of our life."

In this society, Kings were often compared to the Sun.

Baldock continued, "Prepare for a new life, an afterlife, man. Throw up thy eyes and heart and hand to Heaven's immortal throne.

"Pay nature's debt — death — with a cheerful countenance.

"We can summarize all our life-lessons to this: We learn that we will die, sweet Spenser; therefore, we all live, Spenser, we all live to die, and we rise to fall."

He was referring to the Wheel of Fortune. As the Wheel turns, those on the bottom rise high and those at the top fall low.

"Come, come, keep these sermons for when you come to the place appointed for your deaths," Rice ap Howell said. "Keep those sermons for your last words. You, and such as you are, have made 'wise' work in England. Will your lordships leave?"

"Your lordship, I trust, will remember me," the mower said. "Will you reward me?"

"Remember thee, fellow?" Rice ap Howell said. "Of course! What else? Follow me to the town."

They exited.

CHAPTER 5
— 5.1 —
[Scene 20]

On 20 January 1327, King Edward II, the Earl of Leicester, the Bishop of Winchester, and Sir Trussel met in a room of Killingworth Castle in Warwickshire.

The Earl of Leicester said to King Edward II, "Be patient, my good lord, cease to lament. Imagine that Killingworth Castle is your court, and that you are staying here for a while for pleasure, not because of compulsion or necessity."

"Earl of Leicester, if gentle words might comfort me, thy speeches long ago would have eased my sorrows, for kind and loving have thou always been," King Edward II replied. "The griefs of private men are soon allayed, but not those of Kings. The forest deer, being struck, runs to an herb that closes up the wounds."

People in this society believed that wounded deer would seek out and eat a healing herb named dittany.

He continued, "But when the imperial lion's flesh is gored, he rends and tears it with his wrathful paw, and highly scorning that the lowly earth should drink his blood, rears up into the air.

"And so it fares with me, whose dauntless mind the ambitious Mortimer would seek to curb, as does that unnatural Queen, false Isabel, who thus has shut up and caged me in a prison.

"For such outrageous, excessive passions overwhelm my soul, as with the wings of rancor and disdain, I am soaring up very often to Heaven, to complain to the gods against them both.

"But when I recall in my mind that I am a King, I think I should revenge the wrongs that Mortimer and Isabel have done to me.

"But what are Kings, when royal authority is gone, but mere shadows on a sunny day? My nobles rule; I bear the name of King; I wear the crown; but I am controlled by them — by Young Mortimer and my unfaithful Queen, who stains my nuptial bed with infamy while I am lodged within this cave of cares and worries, where sorrow at my elbow always attends and waits on me, to accompany my heart with sad laments that bleed within me for this my strange transformation from King to prisoner.

"But tell me, must I now resign my crown in order to make usurping Mortimer a King?"

"Your grace is mistaken," the Bishop of Winchester said. "It is for England's good, and for princely Edward's right, that we crave the crown."

"No, the crown is for Mortimer's and not Prince Edward's head," King Edward II said, "for Prince Edward is a lamb, surrounded by wolves that in a moment will shorten his life. But if proud Mortimer should wear this crown, may the Heavens turn it to a blaze of quenchless fire."

The mythological sorceress Medea was married to Jason of Jason and the Argonauts fame. When he abandoned her and married Creusa, Medea gave her a crown that burst into flame when she put it on her head.

King Edward II continued, "Or, like the snaky wreath of Tisiphone, may it encircle the temples of his hateful head."

Tisiphone was one of the Furies, who had snakes for hair.

He continued, "So shall not England's vine — the House of Plantagenet — be perished, but Edward's name will survive, although Edward dies."

The vine symbolizes royal lineage.

"My lord, why waste you thus the time away?" the Earl of Leicester said. "Members of Parliament are awaiting your answer. Will you yield your crown?"

King Edward II said, "Ah, Leicester, consider how hardly I can bear to lose my crown and kingdom without cause, in order to give ambitious Mortimer my right — Young Mortimer, who like a mountain overwhelms my bliss. My mind here is murdered in that extreme.

"But what the Heavens appoint I must obey. Here, take my crown; take the life of Edward, too."

He took off his crown, but he held on to it.

He said, "Two Kings in England cannot reign at once. But wait a while. Let me be King until night, so that I may gaze upon this glittering crown. So shall my eyes receive their last moment of contentment, and so shall my head receive the latest honor due to it, and then jointly both my head and eyes shall yield up their wished-for right."

Still not wanting to give up the crown, he said, "Continue always, thou celestial Sun. Never let silent night possess this land. Stand still, you watches of the element."

King Edward II meant that he wanted the Sun, the Moon, and the other planets to stand still and not let time pass. "Watches" are "watchers" or "sentinels" or "timepieces." Most often, the phrase used was "watches of the night," which meant "nighttime." By using "watches of the element," King Edward II was referring to all Heavenly bodies, including the Sun. In this context, "element" means "sky."

He continued, "All times and seasons, rest yourselves at a standstill, so that Edward may be still fair England's King. But day's bright beams do vanish quickly away, and necessarily I must resign my wished-for crown.

"Inhuman creatures, nursed with tiger's milk, why do you greedily open your mouths for your sovereign's overthrow?"

This society believed that babies acquired some of their personal characteristics from their mother's milk. Tigers were known for being cruel, and so anyone who had nursed from a tigress would be cruel.

He continued, "You want to swallow my diadem, I mean, and my innocent life."

He put the crown on his head.

King Edward II continued, "See, monsters, see! I'll wear my crown again. What, don't you fear the fury of your King? But, unfortunate Edward, thou are foolishly mistaken that you can change things. They don't care about thy frowns as they recently did, but instead seek to make a newly elected King."

Parliament would elect the new King.

He continued, "This fills my mind with strange despairing thoughts. These thoughts are martyred with endless torments, and in this torment I find no comfort but that which I get from feeling the crown upon my head, and therefore let me wear it yet a while."

"My lord, the Parliament must have quick news, so therefore tell us whether you resign the crown or not," Sir Trussel said.

King Edward II grew angry and said, "I'll not resign, but while I live —."

He could not finish the sentence due to excess emotion, but he said, "Traitors, be gone, and join with Young Mortimer. Elect, conspire, install

someone else as King, do what you will. Their blood and yours shall seal —
attest to and be the end of — these treacheries.”

“This answer we’ll return to the Parliament,” the Bishop of Winchester said,
“and so, farewell.”

Sir Trussel and the Bishop of Winchester started to leave.

“Call them back again, my lord, and speak to them gently,” the Earl of
Leicester said, “for if they go, Prince Edward shall lose his right to succeed to
the throne.”

“Thou call them back,” King Edward II said. “I have no power to speak.”

“My lord of Winchester, the King is willing to resign,” the Earl of Leicester
said.

“If he is not, let him choose,” the Bishop of Winchester said.

King Edward II said, “Oh, I wish I might, but the Heavens and Earth
conspire to make me miserable. Here, receive my crown.

“Receive it? No, these innocent hands of mine shall not be guilty of so
foul a crime. He of you all who most desires my blood and will be called the
murderer of a King, take it.”

No one wanted to take the crown from King Edward II’s head.

He continued, “Are you moved to pity? Do you pity me? Then send for
unrelenting Mortimer and Isabel, whose eyes being turned to steel will sooner
spark with angry fire than shed a tear.

“Yet wait; for rather than I will look on them, I would rather give up my
crown.

“Here, here!”

He handed over the crown.

He continued, “Now, sweet God of Heaven, make me despise this
transitory pomp that is my earthly life, and make me sit forever enthroned in
Heaven. Come, death, and with thy fingers close my eyes, or if I live, let me
forget myself.”

“My lord —” the Bishop of Winchester began.

The deposed Edward II said, “Don’t call me lord! Go away! Get out of my
sight! Ah, pardon me. Grief makes me lunatic — mad! Don’t let that Mortimer
be named the guardian of and Lord Protector for my son.”

If Young Mortimer were named Lord Protector, he would rule England until the new King — Prince Edward will become King Edward III — came of age.

The deposed Edward II said, "More safety is there in a tiger's jaws than in Young Mortimer's embraces."

He wiped his teary eyes with a handkerchief and then said, "Carry this — wet with my tears, and dried again with my sighs — to the Queen."

He handed over the handkerchief and said, "If with the sight of this she is not moved, return it back to me and dip it in my blood.

"Commend me to my son, and bid him rule better than I. Yet how have I transgressed, unless it be with too much clemency?"

He had allowed Young Mortimer to live rather than have him executed.

"And thus most humbly we take our leave," Sir Trussel said.

The Bishop of Winchester and Sir Trussel exited.

"Farewell," the deposed Edward II said. "I know the next news that they bring will be my death, and welcome it shall be. To wretched men death is felicity — it is happiness."

Someone entered the room.

"Another messenger is coming," the Earl of Leicester said. What news does he bring, I wonder?"

"Such news as I expect," the deposed Edward II said.

The Earl of Berkeley walked over to them.

"Come, Berkeley, come," the deposed Edward II said, "and tell thy message to my naked breast."

He meant that the Earl of Berkeley's message would be a literal stab to his — Edward II's — heart.

"My lord, don't think that a thought so villainous can harbor in a man of noble birth," the Earl of Berkeley said. "To do your highness service and duty and save you from your foes, Berkeley would die."

He gave a letter to the Earl of Leicester, who read it and said to the deposed Edward II, "My lord, the council of the Queen commands that I resign my charge. I will no longer be your keeper."

"And who must keep me now?" the deposed Edward II said.

He asked the Earl of Berkeley, "Must you, my lord?"

"Yes, my most gracious lord," he replied. "It is so decreed."

King Edward II took the letter, looked at it, and said, "Decreed by Young Mortimer, whose name is written here! Well may I rend the name of him who rends my heart."

He tore up the letter and then said, "This poor revenge has somewhat eased my mind. So may his limbs be torn as is this paper. Hear me, immortal Jove, and grant my prayer, too!"

He was using the name "Jove" to refer to God.

"Your grace must go from here with me to Berkeley Castle immediately," the Earl of Berkeley said.

"I will go wherever you want to take me," the deposed Edward II said. "All places are alike, and every earth is fit for burial."

"Treat him well, my lord, as much as lies in you," the Earl of Leicester said. "Treat him as well as you are able to."

"Even so betide my soul as I treat him," the Earl of Berkeley said. "Let my soul be rewarded or punished in accordance with how I treat him."

"My enemy has pitied my condition," the deposed Edward II said, "and that's the reason that I am now being moved from Killingworth Castle to Berkeley Castle."

He was sarcastic; he knew that Young Mortimer did not pity him.

"And does your grace think that Berkeley will be cruel?" the Earl of Berkeley asked.

"I don't know," the deposed Edward II said, "but of this I am sure: Death ends all, and I can die but once. Leicester, farewell."

"Not yet, my lord," the Earl of Leicester said. "I'll see you on your way."

— 5.2 —

[Scene 21]

Young Mortimer and Queen Isabella talked together in a room at the royal palace.

"Beautiful Isabel, now we have our desire," Young Mortimer said. "The proud corrupters — the Spensers and Baldock — of the light-brained, frivolous King Edward II have done their homage to the lofty gallows, and the deposed King himself lies in captivity.

"Be ruled by me and take my advice, and we will rule the realm. In any case take heed of childish fear, for now we hold an old wolf — the deposed Edward II — by the ears, an old wolf that, if he is released, will seize upon us both, and seize us all the more grievously, being seized himself.

"Think, therefore, madam, that it is very important for us to raise your son — Prince Edward — to the throne and make him King with all the speed we may, and that I be made Lord Protector over him, for our authority will have the greater sway when we can exercise it under a King's name."

Prince Edward would be able to sign official documents as King of England, and Young Mortimer would be the actual ruler of England as Lord Protector. Young Mortimer was certain that he could persuade Prince Edward to sign the documents that he wanted him to sign. Or Young Mortimer could sign the documents himself as Lord Protector.

"Sweet Mortimer, the life of me, Isabel, be assured that I love thee well, and therefore, as long as the Prince, my son, whom I esteem as dear as these eyes of mine, is safe, decide whatever you will against his father, and I myself will willingly subscribe and agree to it."

Young Mortimer replied, "First I want to hear the news that he has been deposed, and then let me alone to handle him."

A messenger entered the room, carrying letters.

"Letters! From where?" Young Mortimer asked.

"From Killingworth, my lord," the messenger answered.

"How fares my lord the King?" Queen Isabella asked.

"He is healthy, madam, but full of sorrow," the messenger answered.

"Alas, poor soul, I wish that I could ease his grief!" Queen Isabella said.

The Bishop of Winchester entered the room, carrying the King's crown.

Queen Isabella said, "Thanks, gentle Winchester."

She then ordered the messenger, "Sirrah, be gone."

The messenger exited.

"The King has willingly resigned his crown," the Bishop of Winchester said.

"Oh, happy news!" Queen Isabella said. "Send for the Prince, my son."

"Further, before this letter of abdication was sealed, Lord Berkeley came, so that the deposed Edward II now has gone from Killingworth," the Bishop of Winchester said. "And we have heard that Edmund, Earl of Kent, his brother, has laid a plot to set his brother the deposed King free. That is all that I have heard about that plot. The lord of Berkeley is as full of pity for the deposed Edward II as the Earl of Leicester, who had charge of him before."

"Then let some other person be his guardian," Queen Isabella said.

"Leave that to me," Young Mortimer said, and then he motioned for the Bishop of Winchester to leave.

The Bishop of Winchester exited.

Young Mortimer said to Queen Isabella, "Here is the privy seal."

The privy seal was the personal seal of the King of England. Young Mortimer could use the privy seal to sign important documents and letters, such as one directing that someone new guard the deposed King.

He called for some attendants, "Who's there?"

A couple of attendants entered the room.

Young Mortimer ordered, "Call here Sir Thomas Gurney and Sir John Maltravers."

The attendants exited.

He said to Queen Isabella, "To ruin the heavy-headed, foolish Edmund, Earl of Kent's scheme, the Earl of Berkeley shall be discharged, and the deposed King moved to another location, and none but we shall know where he is staying."

"But, Mortimer, as long as Edward II survives, what safety remains for us or for my son?" Queen Isabella asked.

"Tell me, shall Edward II immediately be dispatched and die?" Young Mortimer asked.

"I wish that he would be," Queen Isabella said, "as long as it were not by my means."

"That is enough," Young Mortimer said.

Sir John Maltravers and Sir Thomas Gurney entered the room.

Young Mortimer ordered, "Maltravers, write a letter immediately to the lord of Berkeley from ourself" — Young Mortimer was using the majestic plural — "saying that he will surrender the King to thee and Gurney, and when it is done, we will sign our name."

"It shall be done, my lord," Sir John Maltravers replied.

"Gurney," Young Mortimer said.

"My lord," Sir Thomas Gurney replied.

"If thou intend to be raised in fortune by me, Mortimer, who now makes Fortune's wheel turn as he pleases, seek all the means thou can to make the deposed King Edward II droop, and give him neither a kind word nor a good look," Young Mortimer said.

He wanted Sir John Maltravers and Sir Thomas Gurney to treat the deposed Edward II badly.

"I promise you I will, my lord," Sir Thomas Gurney replied.

"And this order is more important than the rest," Young Mortimer said. "Because we hear that Edmund, Earl of Kent, schemes to free the deposed King Edward II, move the deposed King always from place to place by night until he comes at last to Killingworth, and then from thence back again to Berkeley. And along the way, to make him fret the more, speak harshly to him, and in any case let no man comfort him. If he should chance to weep, do nothing but amplify his grief with bitter words."

"Fear not, my lord," Sir John Maltravers said. "We'll do as you command."

"So, now go away!" Young Mortimer said. "Leave! Ride that way at once."

"Where is this letter going?" Queen Isabella said. "To my lord the King? Commend me humbly to his majesty, and tell him that I labor all in vain to ease his grief and work for his liberty, and give him this as witness of my love."

She gave Sir John Maltravers a jewel.

"I will, madam," he said.

Sir John Maltravers and Sir Thomas Gurney exited.

"Finely faked!" Young Mortimer said. "Continue to act like that, sweet Queen."

Talking together, Prince Edward and the Earl of Kent entered the room.

"Here comes the young Prince Edward with the Earl of Kent," Young Mortimer said quietly.

"The Earl of Kent whispers something in Prince Edward's childish ears," Queen Isabella said quietly.

"If the Earl of Kent has such access to the Prince, our plots and stratagems will soon be dashed," Young Mortimer said quietly.

"Treat Edmund, Earl of Kent, in a friendly way as if all were well," Queen Isabella said quietly.

"How is my honorable Lord of Kent?" Young Mortimer asked loudly.

"In health, sweet Mortimer," the Earl of Kent replied.

He asked Queen Isabella, "How fares your grace?"

"I would be well, if my lord your brother were freed," Queen Isabella answered.

The Earl of Kent understood her to mean "freed from prison," but she meant "freed from life."

"I hear that recently he has resigned his crown," the Earl of Kent said.

"The more my grief," Queen Isabella said.

"And mine," Young Mortimer said.

The Earl of Kent said quietly to himself, "Ah, they are faking their grief!"

"Sweet son, come here," Queen Isabella said to Prince Edward. "I must talk with thee."

"Do thou, being his uncle and the next of blood, expect to be appointed Lord Protector over the Prince?" Young Mortimer asked the Earl of Kent.

"Not I, my lord," the Earl of Kent replied. "Who should protect the son, but she who gave him life — I mean the Queen."

"Mother, don't persuade me to wear the crown," Prince Edward said to Queen Isabella. "Let him — my father — be King; I am too young to reign."

"But be content, seeing it is his highness' pleasure," Queen Isabella said. "Your father wants you to wear the crown."

"Let me just see him first, and then I will," Prince Edward said.

"Yes, do, sweet nephew," the Earl of Kent said.

"Brother-in-law, you know it is impossible," Queen Isabella said to the Earl of Kent.

"Why? Is he dead?" Prince Edward asked.

"No, God forbid!" Queen Isabella replied.

"I wish those words proceeded from your heart!" the Earl of Kent said.

"Disloyal Edmund, do thou favor him, you who were a cause of his imprisonment?" Young Mortimer asked the Earl of Kent.

Previously, Young Mortimer had addressed the Earl of Kent using the respectful "you," but now he was using the less respectful "thou."

"The more reason I have now to make amends," the Earl of Kent said.

"I tell thee, it is not appropriate that one as disloyal as you should be allowed in the company of a Prince," Young Mortimer said to the Earl of Kent.

He then said to Prince Edward, "My lord, he has betrayed the King, his brother, and therefore don't trust him."

"But he repents and sorrows for it now," Prince Edward said.

"Come, son, and go with this gentle lord — Young Mortimer — and me," Queen Isabella said.

"With you I will, but not with Mortimer," Prince Edward replied.

"Why, youngling, are thou so disdainful of Mortimer?" Young Mortimer asked. "Then I will carry thee away by force."

"Help, uncle Kent," Prince Edward said. "Mortimer will wrong me."

Young Mortimer carried Prince Edward away.

"Brother-in-law Edmund, don't interfere," Queen Isabella said. "We are his friends. I am nearer in blood to the Prince than you are, Earl of Kent. I am his mother."

"Sister-in-law, Prince Edward is my responsibility," the Earl of Kent said. "Return him to me."

"Edward is my son, and I will keep him," Queen Isabella said.

Queen Isabella exited.

The Earl of Kent said to himself, "Young Mortimer shall know that he has wronged me. From here I will hasten to Killingworth Castle and rescue the older Edward — Edward II — from his foes, to be revenged on Young Mortimer and thee, the Queen."

— 5.3 —

[Scene 22]

Sir John Maltravers and Sir Thomas Gurney were talking with the deposed Edward II. Some soldiers were present.

"My lord, don't be pensive," Sir John Maltravers said. "We are your friends. Men are ordained to live in misery. Therefore, come; idle delay endangers our lives."

"Friends, where must unfortunate Edward go?" the deposed Edward II said. "Will hateful Mortimer grant no rest? Must I be tormented like the nightly bird — the owl — whose sight is loathsome to all winged fowls? When will the fury of Young Mortimer's mind lessen? When will his heart be satisfied with blood? If my blood will serve, disembowel immediately this breast, and give my heart to Isabel and him. It is the chiefest target they aim at."

"That is not so, my liege," Sir Thomas Gurney said. "The Queen has given us this command to keep your grace in safety. Your emotional outbursts make your griefs increase."

"This treatment makes my misery increase," the deposed Edward II said. "But can my air of life — my breath — long continue when all my senses are distressed with stench? England's King is kept within a dungeon, where I am starved for lack of sustenance. My daily diet is heartbreaking sobs that almost tear the chamber in which my heart resides. Thus lives old Edward not relieved by any, and so I must die, though pitied by many. Oh, water, gentle friends, to cool my thirst and clear my body from foul excrements!"

In this society, the word "excrement" meant both "feces" and "hair." Sir John Maltravers deliberately misunderstood him as meaning "hair."

"Here's gutter water, as we have been ordered to use," Sir John Maltravers said.

He said to the deposed Edward II, "Sit down, for we'll be barbers to your grace."

Some gutters were sewers, so Sir John Maltravers may have been intending to shave the deposed King with water contaminated by feces.

"Traitors, away!" the deposed Edward II said. "What, will you murder me, or choke your sovereign with puddle water?"

"No, but we will wash your face, and shave away your beard," Sir Thomas Gurney said, "lest you be recognized, and so be rescued."

"Why do you try to fight us like this?" Sir John Maltravers asked. "Your labor is in vain."

"The wren may strive against the lion's strength, but all in vain," the deposed Edward II said. "So vainly do I strive to seek for mercy at a tyrant's hand."

Sir John Maltravers and Sir John Gurney washed the deposed Edward II with gutter water and shaved off his beard.

The deposed Edward II prayed, "Immortal powers Who know the painful cares that wait upon my poor distressed soul, oh, aim all your looks upon these daring men who wrong their liege and sovereign, England's King!"

He added, "Oh, Gaveston, it is for thee that I am wronged. For me thou and both of the Spensers died, and for your sakes a thousand wrongs I'll suffer. The Spensers' ghosts, wherever they reside, wish well to mine; and so then bah! For them I'll die."

"Between theirs and yours shall be no enmity," Sir John Maltravers said.

He meant that soon enough the deposed Edward II would be dead, and his ghost and the Spensers' ghosts would be friends.

"Come, come away," he added. "Now put the torches out. We'll enter in by darkness to Killingworth Castle."

The Earl of Kent arrived.

"Guard the King securely," Sir John Maltravers said. "It is the Earl of Kent."

"Oh, gentle brother, help to rescue me," the deposed Edward II pleaded.

"Keep them apart," Sir John Maltravers said. "Thrust the King in among yourselves."

Soldiers surrounded the deposed Edward II to keep him and the Earl of Kent separated.

"Soldiers, let me but talk to him one word," the Earl of Kent said.

"Lay hands upon the Earl of Kent for this assault," Sir Thomas Gurney said. "Arrest him!"

"Lay down your weapons, traitors," the Earl of Kent said. "Give the King to me."

"Edmund, surrender thou thyself to us, or thou shall die," Sir John Maltravers said.

Soldiers seized the Earl of Kent.

"Base villains, why do you seize me like this!" the Earl of Kent said.

"Bind him, and so convey him to the court," Sir Thomas Gurney said.

"Where is the court but here?" the Earl of Kent said. "Here is the King, and I will visit him. Why do you prevent me?"

The court is where lord Mortimer resides," Sir John Maltravers said. "There shall your honor go; and so, farewell."

Sir John Maltravers and Sir Thomas Gurney exited with the deposed Edward II.

"Oh, miserable is that commonwealth where lords keep courts, and Kings are locked in prison!" the Earl of Kent said.

"Why do we delay?" the soldier in command said. "On, sirs, to the court."

"Yes, lead me where you will, even to my death, seeing that my brother cannot be released," the Earl of Kent said.

They exited.

— 5.4 —

[Scene 23]

Alone, Young Mortimer said to himself, "The deposed King must die, or Young Mortimer goes down. The commoners now begin to pity him. Yet he who is the cause of Edward II's death is sure to pay for it when his son is of age, and therefore I will do it cunningly.

"This letter, written by a friend of ours, contains the deposed King's death, yet also bids them save his life."

Although a friend had composed the letter, Young Mortimer had copied the letter so that it was in his own handwriting. Or perhaps he had added in his own handwriting the Latin words "*Pereat iste!*" to the already written letter.

The Latin words mean, "Let him perish!"

Young Mortimer read out loud, "*Edwardum occidere nolite timere, bonum est.*"

He then said, "With the comma after *timere*, this is the translation: '*Fear not to kill the King, it is good that he die.*'"

"But put the comma after *nolite* instead of after *timere*, and there's another sense."

He read out loud, "*Edwardum occidere nolite, timere bonum est.*"

He then said, "With the comma after *nolite*, this is the translation: '*Kill not the King, it is good to fear the worst.*'"

He thought a moment and then said, "This letter, without any comma, shall be sent. That way, once the deposed Edward II is dead, if the letter should be found by chance, Sir John Maltravers and the rest may bear the blame, and we who caused it to be done will be acquitted of responsibility.

"Within this room is locked the messenger who shall convey it, and perform the rest. And by a secret token that he bears, he shall be murdered when the deed is done."

The token could be a ring that Sir Thomas Gurney and Sir John Maltravers would recognize. The token would show that the letter is genuine.

Young Mortimer said loudly, "Lightborn, come forth!"

Lightborn entered the hall.

107

"Are thou still as resolute as thou were before?" Young Mortimer asked.

"What else, my lord?" Lightborn replied. "Of course, I will be — and far more resolute."

"And have thou planned how to accomplish it?" Young Mortimer asked.

"Yes, yes, and none shall know how he died," Lightborn said.

Lightborn knew ways of killing a man that would not leave evidence of how he was killed.

"But when you see his looks, Lightborn, thou will relent," Young Mortimer said.

"Relent?" Lightborn said. "Ha, ha! I am much accustomed to relent."

He was sarcastic: He was NOT accustomed to relent and show mercy. In addition, he was punning. In this society, one meaning of the word "relent" was "dissolve," and he was much accustomed to dissolve poisons in drinks.

"Well, do it bravely and well, and be secret," Young Mortimer said.

"You shall not need to give me instructions," Lightborn said. "This is not the first time I have killed a man. I learned in Naples how to poison flowers so that anyone who smells them dies, to strangle with a piece of linen thrust down the throat, to pierce the windpipe with a needle's point, or, while one is asleep, to take a quill — a small tube — and blow a little poison powder in his ears; or open his mouth, and pour quicksilver down his throat."

Quicksilver is mercury, a poisonous metal that is a liquid at room temperature.

He added, "But yet I have a better way of killing a man than these."

"What's that?" Young Mortimer asked.

"Nay, you shall pardon me for not telling you," Lightborn said. "None shall know my tricks."

"I don't care how you kill him, as long as it is not spied," Young Mortimer said.

He handed Lightborn a letter and said, "Deliver this to Sir Thomas Gurney and Sir John Maltravers. At every ten miles' end, thou will have a horse."

A fresh horse every ten miles would enable Lightborn to ride quickly.

Young Mortimer then said, "Take this."

He gave Lightborn a token, and then said, "Leave, and never see me anymore!"

"No?" Lightborn said, surprised.

"No," Young Mortimer said, "unless thou bring me news of Edward II's death."

"That I will quickly do," Lightborn said. "Farewell, my lord."

Lightborn exited.

Alone, Young Mortimer said to himself, "The Prince I rule, the Queen I command, and with a lowly bow to the ground the proudest lords salute me as I pass. I seal official documents. I cancel official documents. I do whatever I want. I am feared more than loved; let me be feared, and when I frown, let me make all the court look pale from fear."

In Chapter 17 of *The Prince*, Machiavelli states that it is much safer for a Prince to be feared than loved; however, he points out that a Prince ought to avoid being hated.

Young Mortimer continued, "I view the Prince with Aristarchus' eyes, whose looks were as a whipping to a boy."

Aristarchus was an ancient scholar, severe critic, and harsh schoolmaster. According to Young Mortimer, a harsh glance from Aristarchus to a young pupil was like a whipping to the pupil.

Young Mortimer continued, "They thrust upon me the Protectorship of Prince Edward — who is soon to be King Edward III — and they beg me to accept that which I desire. The Kings' Council begs me to be Lord Protector, which is what I want.

"While at the council table, grave enough, and not unlike a 'bashful' — hypocritical — Puritan, first I complain of weakness, saying that the Protectorship of Prince Edward is *onus quam gravissimum*."

The Latin means "the heaviest of burdens."

He continued, "I do that until, being interrupted by my friends, *suscepi* that *provinciam* — or 'I have accepted that office of government' — as they term it. And to conclude, I am Lord Protector now.

"Now all is safe and secure: The Queen and I, Young Mortimer, shall rule the realm and the young King Edward III, and none shall rule us.

"My enemies I will plague, my friends I will promote to high office. And whatever I wish to command, who dares to check or restrain me?

"*Maior sum quam cui possit Fortuna nocere.*"

The Latin, from Ovid's *Metamorphoses*, Book 6, line 195, states, "I am too great for Lady Fortune to harm." The quotation is ominous for Young

Mortimer because in the *Metamorphoses* Niobe says it as she boasts of her seven sons and seven daughters while pointing out that the goddess Latona has only two children: Apollo and Diana. Shortly afterward, to punish Niobe's excessive pride, Apollo and Diana kill all of Niobe's seven sons and seven daughters.

Young Mortimer continued, "And that this should be the coronation day pleases me and Isabel the Queen."

Prince Edward was crowned King Edward III on 1 February 1327.

Trumpets sounded, and Young Mortimer said, "The trumpets sound; I must go take my place."

The young King Edward III, the Bishop of Canterbury, the Champion of the King, some nobles, and Queen Isabella entered the hall.

The ceremonial role of the Champion of the King was to challenge to single combat anyone who disputes the King's right to be King.

"Long live King Edward III, by the grace of god, King of England and Lord of Ireland!" the Bishop of Canterbury said.

The Champion of the King said, "If any Christian, heathen, Turk, or Jew dares to assert that Edward III is not the true King, and will make good his saying with the sword, I am the champion who will combat him."

"None comes," Young Mortimer said. "Sound, trumpets!"

The trumpets sounded.

"Champion, here's to thee," King Edward III said.

He raised a toast to the Champion of the King.

Queen Isabella said, "Lord Mortimer, now take him to your charge."

Her words meant two things: 1) She was telling Young Mortimer to take charge of the young King Edward III, and 2) She was telling him to pay the Champion of the People.

Young Mortimer took the gilt cup the new King had drunk out of and gave it to the Champion of the King; the cup was his pay.

Some soldiers entered the hall with the Earl of Kent as their prisoner.

"What traitor have we there guarded by soldiers with blades and bills — swords and halberds?" Young Mortimer asked.

"Edmund, the Earl of Kent," a soldier answered.

"What has he done?" King Edward III asked.

"He would have taken King Edward II away forcibly as we were bringing him to Killingworth Castle," the soldier said.

"Did you attempt his rescue, Edmund, Duke of Kent?" Young Mortimer said. "Speak."

"Young Mortimer, I did," the Earl of Kent answered. "He is our King, and thou compel this Prince to wear the crown."

"Strike off his head!" Young Mortimer said. "He shall have martial law."

In this case, martial law meant beheading without a trial.

"Strike off my head!" the Earl of Kent said. "Base traitor, I defy thee!"

King Edward III said to Young Mortimer, "My lord, he is my uncle, and he shall live."

"My lord, he is your enemy, and he shall die," Young Mortimer said.

"Stop, villains!" the Earl of Kent said.

"Sweet mother, if I cannot pardon him, beg my Lord Protector for his life," King Edward III said.

"Son, be content," Queen Isabella said. "I dare not speak a word."

"Nor do I, and yet I think I should command," King Edward III said. "But, seeing I cannot, I'll beg for him."

He then said to Young Mortimer, "My lord, if you will let my uncle live, I will repay it when I come of age."

"It is for your highness' good, and for the realm's," Young Mortimer said.

He then said to the guards, "How often shall I tell you to take him away from here?"

"Are thou King?" the Earl of Kent asked. "Must I die at thy command?"

"At our command," Young Mortimer said. "Once more, soldiers, take him away."

"Our command" could mean the command of Young Mortimer and Queen Isabella, or Young Mortimer could have been using the regal plural.

"Let me but stay and speak," the Earl of Kent said. "I will not go. Either my brother or his son is King, and neither of them thirsts for Edmund's blood. And therefore, soldiers, where will you drag me?"

They dragged the Earl of Kent away, and carried him to the place of execution to be beheaded.

"What safety may I look for at Young Mortimer's hands, if my uncle shall be murdered like this?" King Edward III asked his mother, Queen Isabella.

"Fear not, sweet boy," Queen Isabella replied. "I'll guard thee from thy foes. Had Edmund lived, he would have sought thy death. Come, son, we'll ride a-hunting in the park."

King Edward III asked sarcastically, "And shall my uncle Edmund ride with us?"

"He is a traitor," Queen Isabella said. "Don't think about him. Come."

They exited.

— 5.5 —

[Scene 24]

Sir John Maltravers and Sir Thomas Gurney talked together.

"Gurney, I wonder that the King hasn't died," Sir John Maltravers said. "He is in a vault up to the knees in water, a vault into which the sewers of the castle run. From this vault a damp mist continually arises, which is enough to poison any man, and much more a King who was brought up so tenderly."

"I wonder the same thing, Sir Thomas Gurney said. "I do, Maltravers. Yesternight — last night — I opened the door to throw him food, and I was almost stifled by the stink."

"He has a body able to endure more than we can inflict on him, and therefore now let us assail his mind again for a while," Sir John Maltravers said.

"Send for him to come out from there, and I will make him angry," Sir Thomas Gurney said.

"But wait!" Sir John Maltravers said. "Who is this coming?"

Lightborn entered the room and said, "My Lord Protector greets you."

He gave Sir Thomas Gurney the equivocal letter from Young Mortimer.

"What's this?" Sir Thomas Gurney said, reading the letter. "I don't know how to construe and interpret it."

He handed the letter to Sir John Maltravers, who read it and said, "Gurney, it was deliberately left unpunctuated for the purpose at hand. *'Edwardum occidere nolite timere.'* 'Fear not to kill the King': That's his meaning."

Lightborn showed them Young Mortimer's token and asked, "Do you recognize this token? I must have the deposed King."

"Yes, wait a while," Sir John Maltravers said. "Thou shall have your answer very soon."

Sir John Maltravers and Sir Thomas Gurney went toward the place where the keys to the dungeon were hanging and talked quietly together so that Lightborn could not hear them.

"This villain's sent to murder the deposed King," Sir John Maltravers said.

"I thought as much," Sir Thomas Gurney replied.

"And when the murder's done, see how he must be handled for his labor," Sir John Maltravers said.

He read quietly to Sir Thomas Gurney from Young Mortimer's letter: '*Pereat iste!*'"

Translated: "Let him perish!"

They understood what the Latin means: Kill Lightborn after Lightborn had killed the deposed Edward II.

Sir John Maltravers said quietly to Sir Thomas Gurney, "Let him have the King."

He then said out loud to Lightborn, "Of course! Here are the keys, and this is the pit where the deposed Edward II is staying. Do as you are commanded by my lord, Young Mortimer."

"I know what I must do," Lightborn said. "You two leave, yet don't be far off; I shall need your help. See that in the next room I have a fire, and get me a spit, and let it be red-hot."

"Very well," Sir John Maltravers said.

"Do you need anything besides those things?" Sir Thomas Gurney asked.

"What else?" Lightborn said, thinking. "A feather bed."

"That's all?" Sir Thomas Gurney asked.

"Yes, yes," Lightborn said. "So, when I call you, bring them in."

"Don't be afraid that we won't," Sir John Maltravers said.

"Here's a torch to take when you go into the dungeon," Sir Thomas Gurney said, giving Lightborn a torch.

Sir John Maltravers and Sir Thomas Gurney exited.

"So, now I must go about this business," Lightborn said. "Never has there been any King as finely handled as this King shall be."

He opened the entrance to the dungeon, smelled the stench, and said, disgusted, "Foh, here's a place indeed, I say with all my heart."

In the dungeon, the deposed Edward II asked, "Who's there? What light is that? Why have thou come?"

"To comfort you and bring you joyful news," Lightborn said.

The deposed Edward II came out of the dungeon.

"Poor Edward finds small comfort in thy looks," the deposed Edward II said. "Villain, I know thou have come to murder me."

"To murder you, my most gracious lord?" Lightborn said. "Far is it from my heart to do you harm. The Queen sent me to see how you were treated, for she relents at this your misery. And what eyes can refrain from shedding tears to see a King in this most piteous state?"

"Do thou weep already?" the deposed Edward II said. "Listen a while to me, and then thy heart, even if it were as Gurney's is or as Maltravers' is, hewn from the rock of the Caucasus Mountains, yet thy heart will melt before I have finished my tale.

"This dungeon where they keep me is the cesspool wherein the filth of all the castle falls."

The toilets were above the dungeon and human waste fell into the dungeon where the deposed Edward II was kept.

"Oh, villains!" Lightborn said.

"And there in mire and puddle I have stood these ten days' time," the deposed Edward II said, "and lest I should sleep, someone plays continually upon a drum. They give me bread and water, although I am a King. The result is that, for lack of sleep and sustenance, my mind's disturbed, and my body's numbed, and whether I have limbs or not, I don't know.

"Oh, I wish my blood had dropped out from every vein, as does this water from my tattered robes.

"Tell Isabel, the Queen, that I did not look like this, when for her sake I ran at tilt and jousted in France, and there unhorsed the Duke of Cleremont."

"Oh, speak no more, my lord; this breaks my heart," Lightborn said, bringing in the featherbed. "Lie on this bed, and rest yourself a while."

"These looks of thine can harbor nothing but death," the deposed Edward II said. "I see my tragedy and destruction written in thy brows. Yet wait a while, forbear thy bloody hand, and let me see the stroke before it comes, so that even then at the moment when I shall lose my life, my mind may be more steadfast on my God."

"Why is your highness mistrusting me like this?" Lightborn asked.

"Why are thou lying to me like this?" the deposed Edward II asked.

"These hands were never stained with innocent blood," Lightborn lied. "Nor shall they now be tainted with a King's blood."

"Forgive my thought for having such a thought," the deposed Edward II said. "I have one jewel left; receive thou this."

He gave a jewel to Lightborn; it may have been the jewel that Queen Isabella had sent him.

He continued, "Still I am afraid, and I don't know what's the cause, but every joint shakes as I give the jewel to thee. Oh, if thou harbor murder in thy heart, let this gift change thy mind, and save thy soul. Know that I am a King — oh, at that name I feel a Hell of grief! Where is my crown? Gone, gone, and do I remain alive?"

Many Kings who lose their crowns end up dead quickly.

"You're exhausted from being up much too long, my lord," Lightborn said. "Lie down and rest."

"Except that grief keeps me awake, I would sleep," the deposed Edward II said. "For the past ten days, these eyelids of mine have not closed. Now as I speak they fall, and yet with fear open again. Oh, why do thou sit here?"

"If you mistrust me, I'll leave, my lord," Lightborn said.

"No, no, for if thou mean to murder me, thou will return again," the deposed Edward II said. "So therefore stay."

He slept.

"He sleeps," Lightborn said.

Waking, the deposed Edward II said, "Oh, let me not die yet. Wait! Oh, wait a while!"

"How are you now, my lord?" Lightborn asked.

"Something continually buzzes and whispers in my ears and tells me that if I sleep I will never wake," the deposed Edward II said. "This fear is that which makes me tremble like this. Therefore, tell me: Why have thou come?"

"To rid thee of thy life," Lightborn said.

He raised his voice and called, "Maltravers, come."

Sir John Maltravers entered, carrying the red-hot spit.

"I am too weak and feeble to resist," the deposed Edward II said. "Assist me, sweet God, and receive my soul!"

"Run and get the table," Lightborn said.

Sir John Maltravers and Sir Thomas Gurney brought in a table.

"Oh, spare me, or kill me quickly," the deposed Edward II said.

"So, lay the table down on Edward II, and stamp on it, but not too hard, lest you bruise his body."

They assaulted the deposed Edward II by putting the table on him, and then stamping on it and crushing him. Edward II screamed and died.

According to some chroniclers, the red-hot spit was inserted into the deposed King's rectum, thereby cooking his insides and killing him.

"I am afraid that this cry will raise the town; therefore, let us take to horse and ride away," Sir John Maltravers said.

"Tell me, sirs, was it not bravely and excellently done?" Lightborn asked.

"Excellently well," Sir Thomas Gurney said. "Take this for thy reward."

Sir Thomas Gurney stabbed Lightborn, killing him, and then he said, "Come, let us cast Lightborn's body in the moat and take the deposed King's body to Young Mortimer, our lord. Let's go!"

— 5.6 —

[Scene 25]

Young Mortimer and Sir John Maltravers talked together.

"Is it done, Maltravers, and is the murderer dead?" Young Mortimer asked.

"Yes, my good lord," Sir John Maltravers asked. "I wish that it were undone!"

"Maltravers, if thou now grow penitent," Young Mortimer replied, "I'll be thy ghostly father; therefore, choose whether thou will keep this secret or else die by the hand of me, Mortimer."

A ghostly father is 1) a priest who can listen to the confessions of sins by someone who is about to die, or 2) someone who can make a person a ghost by killing him.

"Sir Thomas Gurney has fled, my lord, and he will, I fear, betray us both; therefore, let me flee," Sir John Maltravers said.

"Flee to the savages!" Young Mortimer said. "Flee beyond the boundaries of civilization!"

"I humbly thank your honor," Sir John Maltravers said, and then he exited.

Alone, Young Mortimer said, "As for myself, I stand like Jove's huge tree, the oak, and others are only shrubs compared to me. All tremble at my name, and I fear none. Let's see who will dare to impeach me for his death!"

Queen Isabella entered the room and said, "Ah, Mortimer, the King my son has received news that his father's dead, and that we have murdered him!"

As Sir John Maltravers had feared, Sir Thomas Gurney had talked about the murder of the deposed Edward II.

"So what if we have?" Young Mortimer said. "The King is still a child."

Queen Isabella said, "Yes, yes, but he tears his hair, and wrings his hands, and he vows to be revenged upon us both. Into the council chamber he has gone, to ask for the aid and assistance of his peers.

"Ah, me, see where he comes, and they with him.

"Now, Mortimer, begins our tragedy and destruction."

King Edward III entered the scene, accompanied by some lords.

"Fear not, my lord," the first lord said. "Know that you are a King."

"Villain!" King Edward III said to Young Mortimer.

"How are you now, my lord?" Young Mortimer asked.

"Don't think that I am frightened by thy words," King Edward III said. "My father's murdered through thy treachery, and thou shall die, and on his mournful coffin thy hateful and accursed head shall lie to witness to the world that by thy means his Kingly body was too soon interred."

"Don't cry, sweet son," Queen Isabella said.

"Don't forbid me to cry," King Edward III replied. "He was my father, and if you had loved him half as well as I, you could not bear his death calmly like this. But you, I fear, conspired with Young Mortimer."

"Why don't you speak to my lord the King?" the first lord asked Young Mortimer.

"Because I think it beneath me to be accused," Young Mortimer replied. "Who is the man who dares to say I murdered him?"

"Traitor, in me my loving father speaks, and plainly says that it was thou who murdered him," King Edward III said.

Now that King Edward II was dead, Prince Edward was truly King Edward III. He could speak with all the authority of a legitimate King.

"But has your grace no other proof than this?" Young Mortimer asked.

"Yes, if this is the handwriting of Mortimer," King Edward III answered, displaying the equivocal letter that Young Mortimer had sent to Sir John Maltravers and Sir Thomas Gurney.

"False Gurney has betrayed me and himself," Young Mortimer whispered to Queen Isabella.

She whispered back, "I feared as much; murder cannot be hidden."

"It is my handwriting," Young Mortimer said to King Edward III. "What do you conclude by that?"

"That thou did send a murderer to my father," King Edward III said.

"What murderer?" Young Mortimer said. "Bring forth the man I sent."

"Ah, Mortimer, thou know that he is slain," King Edward III said, "and so shall thou be, too."

He asked his attendants, "Why is he still here? Take him to a hurdle, and drag him to the place of execution. Hang him, I say, cut his body into quarters and display his quarters, and bring his head back quickly to me."

The hurdle was a wooden frame or sled that would drag Young Mortimer to the place of execution. He would be hung, and then his body would be cut into four quarters and his head cut off.

"For my sake, sweet son, pity Mortimer!" Queen Isabella said.

"Madam, don't beg for my life," Young Mortimer said. "I would rather die than plead for my life to a paltry boy."

"Hence with the traitor, with the murderer!" King Edward III ordered.

"Base Lady Fortune," Young Mortimer said, "now I see that in thy wheel there is a point to which when men aspire, they tumble headlong down. That point I touched, and seeing there was no place to mount up higher, why should I grieve at my declining fall?

"Farewell, fair Queen, weep not for Mortimer, who scorns the world and, as a traveller, goes to discover countries yet unknown."

"What!" King Edward III said, angry at his orders being slowly carried out. "Do you allow the traitor to delay?"

Young Mortimer exited, guarded by the first lord.

"As thou received thy life from me, don't spill the blood of gentle Mortimer," Queen Isabella said to King Edward III, her son.

"This argues that you spilt my father's blood, else you would not be begging for me to spare Mortimer," King Edward III said.

"I spill your father's blood?" Queen Isabella said. "No!"

"Yes, madam, you, for so the rumor runs," King Edward III said.

"That rumor is untrue," Queen Isabella said. "Because I love thee, this rumor has been fabricated against poor Isabel."

"I do not think her so unnatural as to kill my father, her husband," King Edward III said to his lords. His mother's tears were affecting him.

"My lord, I fear it will prove to be all too true that she is involved in your father's death," the second lord said.

"Mother, you are suspected in his death, and therefore we commit you to the Tower of London until further investigation may be made thereof," King Edward III said. "If you are guilty, don't think that you will find me slack or pitiful, although I am your son."

"Nay, you are committing me to my death, for I have lived too long when my son thinks to cut short my days," Queen Isabella said.

"Away with her!" King Edward III ordered. "Her words cause these tears, and I shall pity her if she speaks again."

"Shall I not mourn for my beloved lord, and with the rest accompany him to his grave?" Queen Isabella said.

Which "beloved lord" did she wish to mourn for? King Edward II? Or Young Mortimer?

"Thus, madam, it is the King's will that you shall go from here," the second lord said.

"He has forgotten me," Queen Isabella said. "Wait, I am his mother."

"Saying that will do you no good," the second lord said. "Therefore, gentle madam, go."

"Then come, sweet death, and rid me of this grief," Queen Isabella said.

She exited, attended by some lords.

The first lord returned, carrying the head of Young Mortimer.

"My lord, here is the head of Mortimer," he said.

King Edward III said, "Go fetch my father's coffin, where Young Mortimer's head shall lie, and bring me my funeral robes.

"Accursed head, if I could have ruled thee then, as I do now, thou had not hatched this monstrous treachery!

"Here comes the coffin. Help me to mourn, my lords.

"Sweet father, here unto thy murdered ghost I offer up this wicked traitor's head. Let these tears, falling from my eyes, be witness of my grief and innocence."

NOTES

— 2.5 —

The life dates of Piers Gaveston, 1st Earl of Cornwall, are c. 1284 – 19 June 1312.

His wife, Lady Margaret de Clare, survived him, remarried, and died on 9 April 1342 at age 48. She was born on 12 October 1293.

— 4.2 —

[Scene 15]

This is a modern description of the game called Prisoner's Base:

Prisoner's Base

"This English game of chase and tag was banned in the 1300s by King Edward III. Before the twentieth century, the game was known as 'Chevy Chase' or 'Chivy.'

"Object of the Game: The team with the most prisoners at the end of the time limit wins.

"You will need: A minimum of ten players. A stick or chalk. Large playing area.

How it was played: The group was divided in half and a line of chalk was placed down the middle between the two teams. About 20-30 feet behind each team a large square (prison) was drawn on the ground using chalk. Each team picked one person to be the prisoner of the other team (usually someone who could run fast). Then each team would try to free their prisoner by sending a team member to the prison through the opposing team to bring him/her back without being captured by a member of the opposing team. If the person attempting to rescue their own prisoner made it to the prison through the opposing team without being caught, he/she was safe while in the prison and could pick their own time to run with the prisoner back to their own side of the line. If the opposing team caught the team member, the team member also became a prisoner needing rescue. So each team was busy both trying to rescue their own prisoners and protect the prisoner(s) from the opposite side from being rescued. At the end of time, the team with the most prisoners won."

Source: "Medieval Games and Recreation: Games Played in the Middle Ages. (Outdoor entertainment during the middle ages centered around the Village Green.)" Accessed 3 October 2018.

http://castle.eiu.edu/reading/MEDIEVALGAMES.pdf

Notes:

The above is lightly edited.

The letters "eiu" mean Eastern Illinois University.

— 5.5 —

[Scene 24]

Edward II's Dungeon

According to the historian Raphael Holinshed, the deposed Edward II was kept for a while in *"a chamber over a foul filthy dungeon, full of dead carrion, trusting so to make an end of him, with the abominable stench thereof* [...]."

Note: I modernized the spelling.

Source: Raphael Holinshed's *Chronicles of England, Scotland, and Ireland,* Volume 2 (New York: AMS Press, 1965). Page 586.

Christopher Marlowe makes the deposed Edward II's lodging worse by having him live under the castle's toilets rather than above a foul dungeon. The deposed Edward II is up to his knees in sewage water.

Edward II's Death

"Whereupon when they saw that such practices would not serve their turn, they came suddenly one night into the chamber where he lay in bed fast asleep, and with heavy featherbeds or a table (as some write) being cast upon him, they kept him down and withal put into his fundament an horn, and through the same they thrust up into his body an hot spit, or (as others have) through the pipe of a trumpet, a plumber's instrument of iron made very hot, the which passing up into his entrails, and being rolled to and fro, burnt the same, but so as no appearance of any wound or hurt outwardly might be once perceived. His cry did move many within the castle and town of Berkeley to compassion, plainly hearing him utter a wailful [wailing] noise, as the tormentors were about to murder him, so that divers [many people] being awakened therewith (as they themselves confessed) prayed heartily to God to receive his soul, when they understood by his cry what the matter meant."

Note: I modernized the spelling.

Source: Raphael Holinshed's *Chronicles of England, Scotland, and Ireland,* Volume 2 (New York: AMS Press, 1965). Page 587.

APPENDIX A: ABOUT THE AUTHOR

It was a dark and stormy night. Suddenly a cry rang out, and on a hot summer night in 1954, Josephine, wife of Carl Bruce, gave birth to a boy — me. Unfortunately, this young married couple allowed Reuben Saturday, Josephine's brother, to name their first-born. Reuben, aka "The Joker," decided that Bruce was a nice name, so he decided to name me Bruce Bruce. I have gone by my middle name — David — ever since.

Being named Bruce David Bruce hasn't been all bad. Bank tellers remember me very quickly, so I don't often have to show an ID. It can be fun in charades, also. When I was a counselor as a teenager at Camp Echoing Hills in Warsaw, Ohio, a fellow counselor gave the signs for "sounds like" and "two words," then she pointed to a bruise on her leg twice. Bruise Bruise? Oh yeah, Bruce Bruce is the answer!

Uncle Reuben, by the way, gave me a haircut when I was in kindergarten. He cut my hair short and shaved a small bald spot on the back of my head. My mother wouldn't let me go to school until the bald spot grew out again.

Of all my brothers and sisters (six in all), I am the only transplant to Athens, Ohio. I was born in Newark, Ohio, and have lived all around Southeastern Ohio. However, I moved to Athens to go to Ohio University and have never left.

At Ohio U, I never could make up my mind whether to major in English or Philosophy, so I got a bachelor's degree with a double major in both areas, then I added a Master of Arts degree in English and a Master of Arts degree in Philosophy. Yes, I have my MAMA degree.

Currently, and for a long time to come (I eat fruits and veggies), I am spending my retirement writing books such as *Nadia Comaneci: Perfect 10*, *The Funniest People in Dance*, *Homer's* Iliad: *A Retelling in Prose*, and *William Shakespeare's* Othello: *A Retelling in Prose*.

By the way, my sister Brenda Kennedy writes romances such as *A New Beginning* and *Shattered Dreams*.

APPENDIX B: SOME BOOKS BY DAVID BRUCE

Retellings of a Classic Work of Literature

Arden of Faversham: *A Retelling*

Ben Jonson's The Alchemist: *A Retelling*

Ben Jonson's The Arraignment, or Poetaster: *A Retelling*

Ben Jonson's Bartholomew Fair: *A Retelling*

Ben Jonson's The Case is Altered: *A Retelling*

Ben Jonson's Catiline's Conspiracy: *A Retelling*

Ben Jonson's The Devil is an Ass: *A Retelling*

Ben Jonson's Epicene: *A Retelling*

Ben Jonson's Every Man in His Humor: *A Retelling*

Ben Jonson's Every Man Out of His Humor: *A Retelling*

Ben Jonson's The Fountain of Self-Love, or Cynthia's Revels: *A Retelling*

Ben Jonson's The Magnetic Lady, or Humors Reconciled: *A Retelling*

Ben Jonson's The New Inn, or The Light Heart: *A Retelling*

Ben Jonson's Sejanus' Fall: *A Retelling*

Ben Jonson's The Staple of News: *A Retelling*

Ben Jonson's A Tale of a Tub: *A Retelling*

Ben Jonson's Volpone, or the Fox: *A Retelling*

Christopher Marlowe's Complete Plays: Retellings

Christopher Marlowe's Dido, Queen of Carthage: *A Retelling*

Christopher Marlowe's Doctor Faustus: *Retellings of the 1604 A-Text and of the 1616 B-Text*

Christopher Marlowe's Edward II: *A Retelling*

Christopher Marlowe's The Massacre at Paris: *A Retelling*

Christopher Marlowe's The Rich Jew of Malta: *A Retelling*

Christopher Marlowe's Tamburlaine, Parts 1 and 2: *Retellings*

Dante's Divine Comedy: *A Retelling in Prose*

Dante's Inferno: *A Retelling in Prose*

Dante's Purgatory: *A Retelling in Prose*

Dante's Paradise: *A Retelling in Prose*

The Famous Victories of Henry V: *A Retelling*

From the Iliad *to the* Odyssey: *A Retelling in Prose of Quintus of Smyrna's* Posthomerica

George Chapman, Ben Jonson, and John Marston's Eastward Ho! *A Retelling*

George Peele's The Arraignment of Paris: *A Retelling*

George Peele's The Battle of Alcazar: *A Retelling*

George Peele's David and Bathsheba, and the Tragedy of Absalom: *A Retelling*

George Peele's Edward I: *A Retelling*

George Peele's The Old Wives' Tale: *A Retelling*

George-a-Greene: *A Retelling*

The History of King Leir: *A Retelling*

Homer's Iliad: *A Retelling in Prose*

Homer's Odyssey: *A Retelling in Prose*

J.W. Gent.'s The Valiant Scot: *A Retelling*

Jason and the Argonauts: A Retelling in Prose of Apollonius of Rhodes' Argonautica

John Ford: Eight Plays Translated into Modern English

John Ford's The Broken Heart: *A Retelling*

John Ford's The Fancies, Chaste and Noble: *A Retelling*

John Ford's The Lady's Trial: *A Retelling*

John Ford's The Lover's Melancholy: *A Retelling*

John Ford's Love's Sacrifice: *A Retelling*

John Ford's Perkin Warbeck: *A Retelling*

John Ford's The Queen: *A Retelling*

John Ford's 'Tis Pity She's a Whore: *A Retelling*

John Lyly's Campaspe: *A Retelling*

John Lyly's Endymion, The Man in the Moon: *A Retelling*

John Lyly's Galatea: *A Retelling*

John Lyly's Love's Metamorphosis: *A Retelling*

John Lyly's Midas: *A Retelling*

John Lyly's Mother Bombie: *A Retelling*

John Lyly's Sappho and Phao: *A Retelling*

John Lyly's The Woman in the Moon: *A Retelling*

John Webster's The White Devil: *A Retelling*

King Edward III: *A Retelling*

Mankind: *A Medieval Morality Play* (A Retelling)

Margaret Cavendish's The Unnatural Tragedy: *A Retelling*

The Merry Devil of Edmonton: *A Retelling*

The Summoning of Everyman: *A Medieval Morality Play* (A Retelling)

Robert Greene's Friar Bacon and Friar Bungay: *A Retelling*

The Taming of a Shrew: *A Retelling*

Tarlton's Jests: A Retelling

Thomas Middleton's A Chaste Maid in Cheapside: *A Retelling*

Thomas Middleton's Women Beware Women: *A Retelling*

Thomas Middleton and Thomas Dekker's The Roaring Girl: *A Retelling*

Thomas Middleton and William Rowley's The Changeling: *A Retelling*

The Trojan War and Its Aftermath: Four Ancient Epic Poems

Virgil's Aeneid: *A Retelling in Prose*

William Shakespeare's 5 Late Romances: Retellings in Prose

William Shakespeare's 10 Histories: Retellings in Prose

William Shakespeare's 11 Tragedies: Retellings in Prose

William Shakespeare's 12 Comedies: Retellings in Prose

William Shakespeare's 38 Plays: Retellings in Prose
William Shakespeare's 1 Henry IV, aka Henry IV, Part 1: A Retelling in Prose
William Shakespeare's 2 Henry IV, aka Henry IV, Part 2: A Retelling in Prose
William Shakespeare's 1 Henry VI, aka Henry VI, Part 1: A Retelling in Prose
William Shakespeare's 2 Henry VI, aka Henry VI, Part 2: A Retelling in Prose
William Shakespeare's 3 Henry VI, aka Henry VI, Part 3: A Retelling in Prose
William Shakespeare's All's Well that Ends Well: A Retelling in Prose
William Shakespeare's Antony and Cleopatra: A Retelling in Prose
William Shakespeare's As You Like It: A Retelling in Prose
William Shakespeare's The Comedy of Errors: A Retelling in Prose
William Shakespeare's Coriolanus: A Retelling in Prose
William Shakespeare's Cymbeline: A Retelling in Prose
William Shakespeare's Hamlet: A Retelling in Prose
William Shakespeare's Henry V: A Retelling in Prose
William Shakespeare's Henry VIII: A Retelling in Prose
William Shakespeare's Julius Caesar: A Retelling in Prose
William Shakespeare's King John: A Retelling in Prose
William Shakespeare's King Lear: A Retelling in Prose
William Shakespeare's Love's Labor's Lost: A Retelling in Prose
William Shakespeare's Macbeth: A Retelling in Prose
William Shakespeare's Measure for Measure: A Retelling in Prose
William Shakespeare's The Merchant of Venice: A Retelling in Prose
William Shakespeare's The Merry Wives of Windsor: A Retelling in Prose
William Shakespeare's A Midsummer Night's Dream: A Retelling in Prose
William Shakespeare's Much Ado About Nothing: A Retelling in Prose
William Shakespeare's Othello: A Retelling in Prose
William Shakespeare's Pericles, Prince of Tyre: A Retelling in Prose
William Shakespeare's Richard II: A Retelling in Prose
William Shakespeare's Richard III: A Retelling in Prose
William Shakespeare's Romeo and Juliet: A Retelling in Prose
William Shakespeare's The Taming of the Shrew: A Retelling in Prose
William Shakespeare's The Tempest: A Retelling in Prose
William Shakespeare's Timon of Athens: A Retelling in Prose
William Shakespeare's Titus Andronicus: A Retelling in Prose
William Shakespeare's Troilus and Cressida: A Retelling in Prose
William Shakespeare's Twelfth Night: A Retelling in Prose
William Shakespeare's The Two Gentlemen of Verona: A Retelling in Prose
William Shakespeare's The Two Noble Kinsmen: A Retelling in Prose
William Shakespeare's The Winter's Tale: A Retelling in Prose